D1352203

THE WILL

When Leigh Castle returns to the mansion she grew up in, it is not a happy occasion. Her mother has died, leaving an estate entangled by a questionable will. It is more than reason enough to rekindle the old rivalries among Leigh and her three sisters, Hania, Anastasia and Claudia. When Anastasia is discovered dead at the bottom of an abandoned mine, chilling fear takes hold of the sisters, compounded by suspicious events. But Leigh's return has also afforded her the chance to meet Bradon Lancaster, the engaging young lawyer hired to handle the estate. Despite the circumstances, the attraction they feel is immediate . . .

PATRICIA WERNER

THE WILL

Complete and Unabridged

ULVERSCROFT
Leicester

First published in 1988

First Large Print Edition
published 2005

British Library CIP Data

Werner, Patricia
    The will.—Large print ed.—
    Ulverscroft large print series: romance
    1. Romantic suspense novels
    2. Large type books
    I. Title
    813.5′4 [F]

    ISBN 1–84617–064–8

Published by
F. A. Thorpe (Publishing)
Anstey, Leicestershire

For my sister-in-law, Amy

Life ebbs from me. Those who have gone before me await me. Do they know what is in my heart? These last nine years, I have questioned much, wondering if God will take his vengeance on me. I leave it in His hands. If I am an instrument of His will, then matters will take their course as I think they should.

If He is angry with me, then earthly atonement will be done, and God will stay her hand — my daughter, who knows her heritage, for have I not bred her in my footsteps?

I can surely rest easy, for the Lord knows how I have suffered. My last gesture carries with it the irony that life has forced upon us.

My only doubt, and I confess it here in my journal, in what must surely be my last entry — for how can I expect another good day while this illness claims more and more of me? — my only doubt is that there is one other who knows my secret. I had meant to tell A. of it, but I do not expect her to arrive in time. And can I trust a letter? I think not. For other eyes could peruse a letter not meant for them. I must leave it in her hands, trusting she will know how to remove all obstacles. The other two may wonder, but they will benefit in the end, for are not three parts larger each than if divided by four?

I tire even as I write, and I must stop. I will put away this journal, where I have shared so many thoughts known to no other. My body will soon turn to dust, and so will these pages. But no matter, for what's done is done.

— S.C.

1

The house stood like a sentinel on the side of the hill. Brick and stone rose two stories, with steep gables facing the town below. The tall, narrow windows of the east wing seemed to watch Leigh approach. Juniper trees, thick cholla, and tall yucca dotted the rocky hill. From the heavy gray clouds gathering, Leigh knew it was going to rain, and she shifted to low gear to make the climb before the rain caught her.

Culver City. How odd to be back, although she had known that one day she would return for this very reason. Her stomach muscles tightened as she pulled the little rented Mustang through the iron gates and onto the gravel drive that circled in front of the house. She'd only been back to Culver City once in the nine years since her father had died. Now it was her mother.

When her eldest sister, Hania, called with the news, Leigh had experienced a shock. She had not expected her mother to die. But that was silly — it happened to everyone. It was strange, though, how little grief she felt at the thought of tomorrow's funeral. Still, there was a dryness in her throat as she took in her surroundings. This was supposed to be home, but it always took a while for her to feel that way about it after being away for any length of time. She was more comfortable in her one-bedroom brownstone apartment in New York City than she was in this fourteen-room mansion situated at the edge of the small town where she and her sisters had grown up.

She twisted the steering wheel to park in front of the other cars and looked back at the house. The sprawling wings, with the gables on the top floor, gave the old house the imposing look its architects had striven for. Leigh gave an involuntary shiver. Surely the edifice used to look less dark. But no, it was the same burnt-sienna brick and stone it had always been. The yellow shutters and the trim on the French doors failed to look cheerful.

A curtain fell in a front window, as if someone had been watching just a moment before. The family must be in the living room. Little drops of rain hit her as she climbed out and locked the car. Then pulling her white wool jacket closer around her, she hurried along the drive toward the house.

Light filtered through the oval-shaped leaded glass in the front door. A shadow passed in front of it, and Leigh realized someone must have been standing in the foyer.

There was no sound in the hallway, but she noticed signs of people about. A pair of gray kid gloves lay on the side table under the gilt-edged mirror facing the stairs. An umbrella hung by the crook over the dark-stained oak banister abutting the newel post. Her eyes roamed up to the cathedral ceiling and over the familiar railing along the second-floor hallway. Nothing much seemed to have changed.

She paused in the silent hallway. No one had greeted her, and the house felt alarmingly empty, even though she knew that was not the case. Her throat tightened as she again realized that both her parents were gone now.

She heard voices coming from the living room and headed that way. When she stepped into the room, everyone paused to look at her. Anastasia, her second-eldest sister, rose from a burgundy-colored brocade chair and approached her. Leigh scanned the well-made-up face for any sign of grief as Anastasia said, 'Leigh, darling, how nice to see you.'

She kissed Anastasia's cold cheek, and she felt herself propelled toward the other side of

3

the room, where the family had gathered.

Anastasia was going on. 'Are you tired? How was the drive from El Paso?'

By now her other two sisters had stood, and Leigh noticed how numb with shock they seemed. She moved toward them, but her attention was arrested by the dark man standing next to the marble fireplace at the end of the room. She had never seen him before, and his presence inhibited her natural reactions upon seeing her family. As she looked curiously at him, she was startled by the flicker in his brown eyes.

'Leigh,' Anastasia said, 'this is Braden Lancaster. He's handling Mother's will. Mr. Lancaster, my sister Leigh, who lives in New York.'

Leigh put out her hand automatically. 'How do you do, Mr. Lancaster?'

Dark lashes veiled his eyes for a moment, then he gave Leigh a slightly crooked smile. 'My pleasure,' he said in a pleasant baritone. She turned away quickly, wanting to greet everyone else.

Hania came forward from the white satin sofa facing the window. She was dressed in a soft blue chiffon gown, and her eyes were moist as she greeted Leigh. 'Leigh, dear, it's good to see you.' As Leigh embraced her, she couldn't help but notice how much her eldest

4

sister had aged. There were definite creases in Hania's pale skin above her broad, flat cheekbones. Nevertheless, her affection warmed Leigh — such a contrast to Anastasia's calculating coldness. Hania turned her cheek for Leigh to kiss.

Over Hania's shoulder, Leigh spied her younger sister impatiently waiting by the two wing chairs. Claudia grinned at her.

'Well, my little sister,' Leigh said when Hania moved aside. She reached for Claudia and embraced the tall, lithe woman. With her slim figure and short, dark hair, Claudia retained an athletic appearance. Holding Claudia away from her, Leigh eyed her with mock seriousness. 'Yes, I do believe you improve with age.'

'Hah,' returned Claudia in her confident alto voice. 'Twenty-six is hardly old. But how are you? I think New York agrees with you.' She smiled, though the smudged makeup and the slight pallor of Claudia's usually ruddy skin gave away the reason for this reunion. Leigh realized she was still closer to Claudia than to the other women, even though they hadn't seen each other in quite some time.

Leigh sighed. 'I guess I can't call you the baby of the family anymore.'

'Twerp,' Claudia said affectionately. 'Some group of kids we make.' Leigh smiled wistfully. Ranging from Claudia's twenty-six to Hania's forty-six, they were indeed no longer children. A lump rose in Leigh's throat. Under happier circumstances, they might have appreciated this reunion more, but the death of their mother had cast a grim shadow on their countenances.

A swift glance around the room told Leigh it was still the same as she'd remembered it. Two strips of white cornice molding separated pale-blue walls from a paler-blue ceiling. Hand-crafted oak doors separated the living and dining rooms, and another set of doors led to the west wing of the house, with its sitting room opening onto the patio. The heavy doors were open now, hidden away where they slid into their wall pockets. The rooms were large, and Leigh remembered how huge she had thought this house was when she was a child.

As she turned, she was conscious of Braden Lancaster staring at her. He was dressed in a gray serge suit with tiny threads of a lighter gray running through the material. Leigh noticed the dark eyes, high cheekbones, and the sensual, slightly crooked mouth. She looked away quickly. He seemed to be scrutinizing all the women, and his gaze had finally rested on Leigh.

With one knee bent and one arm resting on

the mantel-piece, he struck a casual pose, but it could not disguise a certain air of self-possession. He exuded magnetism, and Leigh wondered if everyone else in the room sensed it as well.

Hanging above the lawyer, over the mantel, was the familiar portrait of Sybil Castle in her prime. Leigh glanced at it, aware, with a sudden twinge, of how lifelike it seemed. It was very much the way Leigh remembered her mother — the dark, short waves of hair, almost severe, unsmiling eyes, narrow face, an aristocratic tilt to the head. Sybil Castle stood next to a burgundy velvet chair, her fingers extended across the chair back. It seemed almost macabre to be gazing at the portrait of the dead woman now. Leigh looked away from it, wanting to find a chair.

'Where are Richard and Nathan?' she asked, realizing that her older sisters' husbands were missing.

Anastasia shrugged, the strand of pearls rising and falling on the bosom of her perfectly tailored gray silk dress. 'Maybe they're upstairs,' she said, moving through the archway to the dining room to fetch the brandy decanter. Leigh listened to Anastasia's heels clicking on the parquet floor.

'They were looking at the house to see

about repairs,' Anastasia continued. 'I suppose they think that when the estate is settled, we'll most likely sell the house — unless one of us wants to live here.' The statement sounded rather more like a challenge, confirming Leigh's assumption that Anastasia was still a fast mover.

'Anastasia,' Claudia said admonishingly, 'Mother hasn't even been laid to rest; surely you can wait until then to start pawing over the estate.'

Hania turned pink and looked at the carpet. Leigh assumed she and Nathan were still living here. It was like Claudia to take Anastasia on. They had always battled as children. Just then Leigh glanced at Braden Lancaster, who was watching them all intently.

'Really, Claudia,' Anastasia said insolently. 'Don't accuse me of insulting Mother's memory. I was merely answering Leigh's question.'

'Please,' Leigh said, trying to stop an argument before it started. 'Let's not show our worst side to Mr. Lancaster.' Then turning to the lawyer, she said, 'I apologize, Mr. Lancaster. We are all under a strain.'

He shifted his position so that his weight was on the other leg, and Leigh followed the movement with her eyes. 'That's all right,

Miss Castle,' he said. 'But perhaps I should go. I only stopped by to see if you ladies needed anything. I'll go over the will with the immediate family and spouses here following the funeral tomorrow, if that has your approval.' His voice was smooth, controlled.

Anastasia veiled what Leigh knew to be displeasure with a show of hospitality, replacing her dark look with a smile for the lawyer as she moved to stand in front of him. 'Of course, Mr. Lancaster. But won't you have more brandy before you go?'

He bowed his head. 'Thank you, Mrs. Hazlett, but I must be off. It was a pleasure to meet you all.' Anastasia reluctantly let go of her quarry.

'I'll see Mr. Lancaster out,' Leigh found herself saying. Again he smiled that half-crooked smile of his and followed her to the entry hall. As she paused to open the front door, he stopped quite close behind her, and she caught the subtle, tangy scent of his aftershave, which reminded her of fresh limes. He reached around her for the door handle, and her eyes followed the lines of his tailored coat and trousers, taking in the polished black shoes he wore.

Then the door opened, and she gratefully breathed in the fresh air. The clouds had moved farther over the Black Range and only

9

a light dampness remained. He followed her and shut the door behind them.

'Thank you for seeing me out, Leigh,' he said as they went down the steps to the drive. He stopped beside the second car in the drive, a blue-gray Volvo, the color of the rain. She put out her hand.

'Goodbye then,' she said as he took it.

'May I offer my condolences?' he said.

Leigh jerked her mouth involuntarily. 'Thank you.' Then she had a thought. 'When did you become my mother's lawyer? I thought Mr. Tyson used to represent her.'

He smiled, and she noticed a small scar on his upper lip that created a slight unevenness.

'Gregory Tyson was my father's partner,' he said. 'When Mr. Tyson died, my father invited me into the business with him. He handled your mother's will when she revised it nine years ago, and now that Dad's planning to retire . . . ' He let it hang.

'She revised it? I wasn't aware of that.'

'Yes, she did.' He frowned. 'Dad said he was fairly surprised at the time. But she was in good health and under no outside influence. She had simply made up her mind about a number of things. I believe it was nine years ago that your father passed away?'

Leigh nodded. 'What does my father's death have to do with it?'

10

Braden, still frowning, looked at the gravel beneath his feet. 'I'm sorry, I shouldn't have brought it up.' He turned toward his car. 'Until tomorrow, Miss Castle.' She watched him get into his car, wondering why he had switched from her Christian name to Miss Castle. He was a puzzling man.

She looked up. The clouds were coming in again, and she was afraid she would get caught in the downpour, so she quickly returned to the house. As she pushed open the front door, she saw a distant flash of lightning. A roar of thunder seemed to start some miles away, then gather strength before it crashed directly overhead.

Upon entering the living room, she turned to see a young Mexican, in a jacket as white as his teeth, smile and incline his head from where he stood in the arched doorway.

'Carlos will bring in your luggage,' Anastasia said. Apparently the family had agreed to keep the servants until the estate was settled. Of course servants would be needed with the family staying in the house until after the funeral. Leigh wondered if the cook, Mrs. Garcia, still worked here. She would ask about her later.

'I'll get on up. Same room?' She saw Hania start to answer, then defer to Anastasia, who nodded distractedly.

As Leigh climbed the stairs, she felt a chill descend over her. She wondered if the old furnace was going. The one-hundred-year-old house had always been hard to heat, and now that it was November, it would be cold at night. Culver City was close to the Continental Divide, and the crisp mountain air turned to frost in the fall.

Upstairs, Leigh turned left, then stopped to reach for the rheostat on the wall. She turned on the light. The two overhead crystal chandeliers had been converted to electricity early in the century. Indeed, the old house carried with it a sense of history, for several generations had lived here. Her family had bought it when her father, Hawthorne, and his cousin Charlie had made their money leasing land for its mineral rights.

She shook her head. Now that money, which had also accumulated from Hawthorne's success in the copper-mining industry, would be passed on to Leigh and her sisters. Of course it would probably take a lot of time to settle the estate. And she was unsure what the assets were worth. Nearly a million by now, she imagined, not counting the house itself. Though after taxes there would be a lot less left to each heir.

The hallway was the same as it had always been. Thick Berber wool runners with a

12

wine-colored floral pattern led to the bedrooms in the east wing. Leigh went straight ahead to her room. It looked out the gable she had seen below as she had approached the house, and it afforded her a view of the town stretched out to the east. It was raining hard now, nearly dark, although only four o'clock. She hoped the storm would pass quickly. Normally this was such a lovely view of the little old mining town. She took off her jacket and opened the old cedar closet, the fresh scent bringing back another flood of memories.

All parents died, and she supposed everyone always thought they'd be ready for it. But one didn't know what it really felt like until it happened. Mother was gone. It made her feel empty rather than sad, for she had not been overly close to Sybil.

Carlos brought the luggage, and Leigh indicated where to put it. 'Thank you, Carlos,' she said. She shut the door after him, wanting a chance to think in the solitude of her room, her mind reaching back over the years.

Hawthorne Castle had been a flamboyant man. Anastasia took after him, although he had seemed to favor Hania with his love. Mother had seemed to spoil Anastasia, perhaps because Hania was her father's favorite. But the other two girls had been left

13

pretty much to themselves. Sybil had always seemed closer to her church than to her family.

During the past nine years, Sybil had ventured out on her own, Leigh recalled as she fingered her suitcase and sat on the bed. She had traveled to Hawaii and visited Leigh in Rome once. They were probably the most active years of Sybil's life. Leigh shivered and rubbed her arms. Sybil had not seemed anxious to follow her husband to the grave. Perhaps these last years she had been able to do what she really wanted to do.

Leigh pushed away the introspective thoughts, for she disliked becoming morbid. Instead she concentrated on Braden Lancaster, the thought of him causing a slight tremor in her throat. What a strange man to live in a town like this, she mused. He seemed too sophisticated, too sure of himself. She would be more likely to run into a man like that in New York than in Culver City. He couldn't have grown up here when they did; they would have known him in school. She would have to ask him about it. He only seemed about six or eight years older than her twenty-eight years. Then she wondered when she might have the opportunity to speak to him alone.

★ ★ ★

The funeral procession wound out of town along the tree-lined highway heading toward the two cemeteries. On one side of the road, the neat, unornamented Masonic cemetery lay with green sagebrush adorning the plain headstones of the well-kept graves. An avenue of ancient oaks and pines stood guard.

Across the road, where Sybil Castle was laid to rest, tilting crosses and gaudy virgins with outstretched arms blessed the flowered graves set here and there between the muddy roads, in loud contrast to the order of the Masonic graves across the highway. The Castle plot was surrounded with high shrubs and the grass was kept mowed as if to separate the copper-mining baron and his family from their poorer neighbors. Autumn's last leaves littered the ground. In the distance, the road led past the mesa flats and the old silver mine.

Leigh watched tensely as the casket was lowered. Claudia stood stiffly, her lips pressed into a straight line and her brows creased together as if fighting any emotion. Hania sobbed quietly into a handkerchief, her face colorless, as it had been the day before, her broad cheeks pale and ghostly looking. Anastasia wore a heavy black veil, so that

Leigh could not see her eyes, only her dark-red lips, which she moistened every so often.

Obligatory tears were shed. Sybil's friends and acquaintances, people Leigh had not seen for over a decade, stood in clusters, clutching handkerchiefs. But still Leigh did not cry. Instead, a cold, twisted knot seemed to lie in her solar plexus, waiting for she knew not what. She knew she needed an emotional release. When would it come? Her eyes drifted to Braden Lancaster and his father, Henry.

Braden, dressed in a dark suit and gray silk tie, was glowering at the grave. His father's gray head was bowed, his lips mumbling silent prayer. The senior Lancaster had had heart ailments in recent years, and Braden said his dad was retiring soon. Apparently he had already turned over most of his workload to his son. Then she wondered why her thoughts wandered over such trivia. They seized on every oddity as if frightened to linger for long on Sybil herself. Leigh did not want to think about her mother's death. She was not ready to confront it.

A gust of wind blew, and Leigh had to hold on to the beige felt hat she wore. Her medium-brown hair, which usually picked up red highlights in the sun, looked dull in the gray light. The priest raised his voice to be heard over the blustery weather, but Leigh barely listened. She was too keenly aware of the people assembled around the grave. Too many images filled her mind. She couldn't help but compare the people here with their appearance nine years ago at her father's funeral. Many of them seemed more faded. Some, of course, had died or moved on.

She sensed that someone was watching her, and she looked at Braden, whose eyes met hers. He lifted his brows in acknowledgment, and she gave him a quick smile, then lowered her eyes. She had no reason to feel embarrassed, but her pulse beat nervously and she swallowed. She didn't look up for several minutes, until she was sure his glance had left her.

When the funeral was over, Leigh returned to her car, feeling relieved to get out of the wind and away from the depressing surroundings. Claudia climbed in with her, and they followed the other cars back to town. As they pulled out, she noticed Braden and his father getting into the Volvo. Of course they would be coming to the house.

'Look,' said Claudia, pointing to the right after they'd gone a quarter of a mile. 'There's the old shale mine.'

'How would you know?' Leigh teased,

finding relief in an extraneous subject. 'Mother always forbade us to go there.' She winced at the mention of their mother but did not back off from it. They had to learn to speak of her sometime.

'Oh, I went there all right,' Claudia answered.

'I'll bet. Especially when you were sixteen with that Foreman boy.'

'Oh, go on,' Claudia said. It was true. She couldn't deny it. But her attention was drawn to other things in the Mexican part of town through which they were passing.

'There's the old Esqueda place,' she said, pointing to a boxlike adobe with porch and railing leaning toward the curb. 'Looks abandoned now.'

Leigh glanced at it quickly. The grass had grown high, and the windows were dark. 'Isn't that where we used to slide off the roof into a pile of rubber tires?' she asked.

'Yes,' Claudia answered. 'I remember telling on the rest of you because I was too little and I couldn't go along.'

Leigh smiled at the memory.

Mrs. Garcia was in the kitchen, and she squeezed Leigh's hands and embraced her when the two met in the kitchen. There was food and coffee for friends who stopped by. Leigh talked and nodded automatically to their guests, particularly noticing how nervous Anastasia looked. Her gestures, usually flowing and elegant, were flighty, and her voice was too loud.

Finally most of the guests left, and Mrs. Garcia began to clean up. The family assembled in the large dining room around the smoothly polished oval table surrounded by Queen Anne chairs. Braden sat at the head of the table. He looked up at Leigh as she entered the room and then away. She moved to a chair between Claudia, who sat at the foot of the table, and Anastasia, on the right.

Richard Hazlett, Anastasia's husband, in a three-piece navy-blue suit, with his pipe in one hand, stood behind his wife, his fingers drumming on the wainscoting behind him. Across the table, Nathan Hunter, Hania's husband, a slightly balding man in his middle forties, stood straight beside the buffet, which held the silver coffee service. Leigh wondered idly why these two men didn't sit down; there were plenty of chairs.

Braden reached into his jacket pocket and produced the will, which he quickly unfolded. It was a single piece of paper, and after glancing at the company, he began to read it.

'I, Sybil Castle, domiciled and residing in Culver City, Grant County, New Mexico, declare that this is my will and revoke all other wills.' He cleared his throat and continued.

'I am widow of the late Hawthorne Castle, and we have four children: Hania Castle Hunter, Anastasia Castle Hazlett, Leigh Castle, and Claudia Castle.

'I appoint my son-in-law Nathan Hunter executor of this will.' There followed a clause in which the executor was directed to pay medical, funeral and administrative expenses and taxes. Then Braden cleared his throat again.

Suddenly, Leigh tensed, feeling, in the way he jerked his mouth, that something unusual was coming. He went on.

'I give my home and all of my tangible personal property, my entire estate and all its assets to my eldest daughter, Hania Castle Hunter, if she survives me. If she does not survive, I give my personal property, my house and my entire estate to my surviving daughters to be divided equally. In testimony of which I now sign this will, witnessed and so on and so forth.' Braden finished.

Then he placed the paper on the table and looked at the expectant faces turned toward him. 'That is all,' he said quietly.

There was silence.

2

Anastasia was the first to react. She drew herself up sharply, the gold chains that hung down her blue crepe tailored blouse shimmering in the light as she moved. 'What do you mean, Mr. Lancaster?' Her anguished voice pierced the momentary hush.

'Anastasia,' said Nathan from across the table. 'Control your voice. There may still be some neighbors in the house.' He gestured plaintively, meaning that he did not want to have a scene.

Leigh felt her mouth drop halfway open as she glanced at her other sisters. Hania's hand was at her chest, her face ashen. Nathan bent over and whispered something to her. Claudia stared up at Anastasia, whose face was twisted in rage.

Richard Hazlett spoke up. 'We'll contest this will. When was it made?' Braden did the best he could to placate them, but the voices around the table got louder, in spite of Nathan's attempt to shush everyone. Claudia leaned over to say something to Leigh, which she couldn't hear, even though she cupped her ear with her hand to try to catch the

21

words. But by then Braden had regained control of the group.

'Please, please,' he was saying. 'I know this is unexpected. At least, I thought it would be.' He looked around in question, as if any evidence to the contrary were now welcome.

'Of course it is unexpected,' said Anastasia shrilly. Leigh thought she had never seen Anastasia with such lack of poise. She realized then what a calculating woman Anastasia had always been and what a calamity this must be for her. There had not been too many surprises for her in life, at least not surprises that she couldn't turn to her advantage.

But Braden didn't let her continue. He raised the palm of his hand to her and addressed the others. Anastasia was silenced by the sheer force of his gesture and the fact that he was clearly ignoring her. Another unusual circumstance, Leigh noticed. Most men did not readily ignore Anastasia.

'In case any one of you is thinking of contesting this will,' Braden said, 'let me assure you it is quite legal. It was made in the presence of both my father and Gregory Tyson nine years ago. Sybil was in good health and apparently of sound mind. She told my father and Mr. Tyson that she had changed her mind about something and that it was very important to do this. Naturally they did not press her. She just said her reasons were personal.'

'How could she?' Claudia exclaimed. Her face was blotchy now, and she was frowning down at the linen tablecloth.

Leigh herself was as shocked as the others, and she hadn't time to get a grip on her feelings. Her mind took over robotically, recording the scene before her. That the inheritance was going to Hania seemed established. The effect it would have on the rest of them was quite vast, she was sure. She noticed the desperate glint in Richard Hazlett's eye. He and Anastasia must have been counting on their share of the inheritance. Leigh raised an eyebrow in speculation. They lived in grand style, but they seemed rather nervous. Perhaps they had run up debts.

Everyone was moving now. Even the chandelier overhead seemed to sway. Nathan pulled Hania out of her chair, and as she stood, Anastasia glared across the table at her. Leigh took a deep breath. Certainly this was unexpected, and she did not understand why Sybil had bequeathed everything to her eldest daughter. She was unsure what Hania and Nathan's financial needs were. At least now they wouldn't have to move out of the house.

23

Then she pressed her lips together, realizing that her thought was uncharitable.

Leigh felt her head start to spin and decided she needed some air; the room seemed suddenly filled with too much tension. As she pulled herself up and made her way to the closed double doors, she caught Braden's tall form starting to move as well. He said a few words to each person who passed him. Richard Hazlett grabbed him by the arm, his facial muscles rigid.

'My wife and I will see you in your office tomorrow morning. I want to call my lawyer in New York.'

Bradon nodded, unmiffed, Leigh thought, as she watched him from the doorway. But then, what was it to him that four sisters were victims of a lopsided fate? Leigh made her way through the living room. She felt slightly nauseated and hurried toward the front door, past the neighbors talking in low tones at the other end of the room. They were probably speculating about the will. Neighbors — kind and helpful during one's life, vultures at one's death.

She heard a soft tread behind her and turned to see Braden following her. He seemed equally glad to be out of that room. Something like relief showed in his eyes and in the way he relaxed his shoulders.

'Going out?' he asked as he caught up with her in the front hall.

'Yes,' she said. 'I needed some air.'

They walked out the door and down the steps to the drive. She thought Braden was on the verge of accompanying her, but then Nathan Hunter appeared at the top of the steps and called to him. Braden stopped.

Leigh shuddered involuntarily, as if to shake off the charged atmosphere inside. Quietness enveloped her as she headed away from the house. At the end of the drive, she stepped onto the street and turned toward the hill. Then at the end of the road, she walked on the packed dirt of a path that led to the top of a low ridge above the house. She still had on her dress shoes, beige pumps with two-inch heels, so progress was difficult.

She remembered running up this hill as a child. Yes, there was Tree Rock, a place she used to call her own, where a single juniper rose from a large outcropping of rock, reaching upward from the top of the hill. She smiled faintly in reminiscence.

'Leigh,' a voice called. She jumped, her heart beating suddenly as she turned. She hadn't realized anyone was following her. But there, a few yards below her on the dirt path, was Braden, his muscular legs making their way up the hill toward her.

She waited, catching her breath. She still felt queasy from the events just past, and while she knew she should be polite to Braden, she also wanted to pull away, to be alone to sort out her feelings.

'I hope you don't mind if I join you,' he said as he got closer to her. Then he turned and looked back down the hill. 'Quite a view.' From where they stood, the ground fell away into valleys on both sides of the ridge. The town lay to the south and east.

Leigh brushed her hair out of her face, the strands taking on a reddish-gold cast here in the sunset. She turned to look at the rocky hills in the distance on the side away from town. It was quite a view, she had to agree — still, but with a subtle energy. It soothed her to look at it.

She was aware of his presence beside her, and she wondered briefly why he had followed her up here. For a moment neither spoke. Her heartbeat gradually returned to its normal rate, and she realized she had not exerted herself at this high an altitude for some time.

She smiled slowly. 'I used to come here a lot when I was growing up. Of course it's been a long time since I've been back.' She'd come here after her father's funeral too, she recalled as she ran one hand over the old familiar smooth place where she always sat. Then she looked at Braden. 'I meant to ask you, if you don't think I'm being impertinent. You couldn't have gone to school here — we would have known you.' She blushed, thinking he must know she was trying to guess his age. But his grin disarmed her.

'We didn't always live here, but I was born here. When I was five, we moved to El Paso, where my father practiced for fifteen years. Then when he moved back here, I was at college in Washington, so you wouldn't have known me at school. That was when Dad joined Tyson's firm. You probably weren't born yet when I left here a wee tot,' he said.

That crooked smile was not unattractive, she thought. She felt more relaxed now, perhaps because they were away from the house and the rest of the family. Then her smile faded and her thoughts returned to the matter at hand. Braden must have noticed her expression, for a shadow passed over his face as well.

'I wonder,' she said softly.

'About the will,' he said.

'Yes. Why did she do it that way?' She looked at him quizzically. He glanced at her inquiring brown eyes, then lifted his shoulders and let them drop.

'She was quite adamant, the way my father

tells it,' he said. 'He asked her if she had informed the other parties cut out of her previous will, and she was vague about it. Said something about the other girls getting their share. I don't think he knew what she meant.'

'Of course you didn't know us at the time.'

'No,' he said. 'I didn't join the firm until Tyson died a year after that. He and my father did discuss the will with her; of course they had all known each other for many years.'

'Yes,' Leigh said.

He frowned down at the ground, and Leigh had the feeling he wanted to say more. He finally looked at her again and said, 'If I were you, I'd be careful, Leigh. I've heard of things like this happening before.' He shook his head. 'Unequal inheritances usually lead to some unpleasantness.'

Leigh shivered. Her light jacket was not enough cover for a lengthy stay on the mountainside.

'Cold?' he asked, moving nearer, and the concern in his voice made something in her respond.

'Ummm,' she nodded. 'Perhaps we'd better start back.'

As he had moved closer to her, she had noticed the worry lines in his face, which made him look as if he were carrying too great a burden. She had the urge to ask him what it was. But his concern over the will was a bit unsettling. Almost as if his words were a warning. And they carried with them an echo, a dim memory that she hadn't yet put her finger on.

He had forced her to confront the fact that she too feared some unpleasant consequences of her mother's action. Of course, Hania could decide to divide up the estate among her sisters. It would be like Hania to want to share everything equally. But she dismissed the thought as soon as it came into her head. Nathan would never allow it, and Sybil had put him in control by making him executor of the estate. Funny, thought Leigh. She had had no idea that Sybil was so fond of Nathan. But perhaps she considered him a good administrator.

Braden hadn't moved. Instead, he lifted his head and sniffed at the juniper and pine scent that permeated the air. 'It's invigorating up here. I'm surprised I never discovered it myself.'

'Have you spent much time exploring the area?' Leigh asked as they started down. Braden took her arm to help her over the rough spots.

'I've gone to the well-known spots — the

Cliff Dwellings, the City of Rocks.'

'Have you ever driven up to Mogollon?' she asked.

'No,' he said. 'But I've heard of it. An old ghost town up in the mountains. I believe they've finally paved the road up there.'

She nodded. 'Last time I went was with my father on a single-lane gravel road that was washed out in some places. It was almost impossible to pass.'

'I hear it's popular with the artists.'

She smiled. 'Claudia and I used to paint there in the summer.'

'You're an artist?'

Leigh shook her head. 'No, not really. I dabble in watercolors. But Claudia has real talent.'

'I'm sure you're being modest.' She smiled at the tone of his voice. It resonated with encouragement, as if he wanted her to talk more about herself.

They had reached the street again, and Braden let go of her arm. He looked at her feet.

'That's no way to treat those shoes.'

'I would have put on hiking shoes, but I wasn't planning to go far.'

They approached the house. 'Interesting house,' said Braden, looking at the sprawling mansion with its six gables. 'Unusual choice of style for this region,' he said. 'The Norman style is more often seen near sea coasts, especially in the Northeast, it seems to me.'

'I suppose that's why Father bought it,' she said. 'He liked unusual things. It used to be so warm, now it's . . . ' she couldn't quite describe what she felt. 'If only the walls could speak,' she said softly, suppressing a sudden tightness in her throat.

Braden, his hands in his pockets, frowned at the pavement, and Leigh wondered what he was thinking. Perhaps it was the desolation around them that drew her toward him. He seemed such a pillar of strength and confidence, someone to rely on in the midst of the confusion.

Yet she wondered if he were telling them all he knew. She had no reason to doubt that he was being truthful, but his sense of professionalism might prevent him from betraying the confidence of a client. If Sybil had said something to Braden's father indicating why she changed her will and didn't want anyone else to know, Braden would not necessarily repeat what his father had told him, even though he might want to reassure the rest of them now.

And had he just wanted a walk and then followed her up the hill to admire the view? Or had he something else in mind? Suddenly,

Leigh felt nervous, and confused. How silly she was, she told herself, to react this way. But then she realized that reactions were not necessarily normal when one came home for a funeral.

Her mother's death had disturbed her in a way she could not define. Perhaps she was still in shock. Small things made the grief well up inside her, but she could not seem to spill it out. The lace curtains in her bedroom reminded her of her mother shutting the window for her when she went to bed at night; the silver and china in the dining room reminded her of family dinners. The images were strong — photographic impressions of past times, with a reality so great it overwhelmed Leigh to recall them.

If she closed her eyes, she felt as if she were returning to an earlier time — a bittersweet time with worries all of a different kind. A time of camaraderie with Claudia and of arguments with Anastasia, Mother's favorite, when Hawthorne had to make the peace. And Hania, always trying to please. She had been so pious, taking their mother's Catholic teachings more seriously than the rest of the girls.

An era had passed. They were all grown up now. Again she felt her throat tighten, though her eyes remained dry.

'Oh, I wish,' she said and reached for Braden's hand before she knew what she was doing. He seized her hand and drew it upward, covering it with his other hand.

'What do you wish?' he said as they stopped at the entrance to the drive, their heads close enough together that she could feel his warmth.

'I . . . don't know.' Her face fell as the images faded.

He nodded, and she felt him squeeze her hand lightly before he dropped it. She smiled in thanks. The gesture had been somehow reassuring.

Just then Claudia came along the drive. She still had on the gray tweed suit with the green silk blouse she had worn to the funeral. Her short dark hair was a contrast to Leigh's fluffy medium-brown, but there were similarities about their faces. Both had long, straight noses and wide-set eyes. And both had a hint of freckles that peeked out of healthy-looking skin. Claudia's coloring was just a shade darker than Leigh's.

'Mr. Lancaster,' Claudia said hesitantly as she approached. Leigh could see the doubt in Claudia's eyes as she asked, 'What will this mean?'

'Please call me Braden,' he said, his smile open and concerned. 'How do you mean that? Legally, nothing, I'm afraid.'

'The will has no loopholes then?' said Leigh.

'No,' he said, frowning. 'I'm sorry. I realize this must have been a rude surprise for you.'

Claudia spoke up. 'Then you wouldn't advise that we contest the will?'

'He couldn't advise us of anything,' Leigh said, a hint of irritation creeping into her voice. 'He represented our mother. He has to respect the wishes of his firm's client.'

'Oh, of course,' said Claudia, frowning slightly. Leigh felt her irritation grow, in spite of her attempt to control her feelings. She knew Claudia had been trying to save enough money to take a couple of years off from work to return to school. Leigh realized, with a twinge, that she had been contemplating a similar move. She had wanted to spend some time traveling to improve her fluency in French. And she had just begun to learn Russian. A trip to that country . . . But that would have to wait.

'What's happened inside?' asked Leigh, turning her thoughts from where they had been leading.

'Not much,' said Claudia. 'No one is speaking to anyone, especially Hania. She went to her room. Gosh, I wonder what she'll do with everything.' Then she looked embarrassed. 'Oh, what a horrible thing to say. I didn't mean . . . '

'Oh, it's all right,' said Leigh, putting a hand on her sister's arm. 'I think we all wonder the same thing. And I don't know what she'll do with everything, really. She and Nathan will continue to live here, I imagine.'

Claudia shrugged. 'It would be enough money to let you do what you wanted for a while,' she said. Then she bit her lip. 'Oh, I don't mean to sound envious.' Tears sprang to her eyes, and she wiped them with the back of her hand. 'But I feel so, so cut off . . . '

'Claudia,' said Leigh, putting her arm around the girl's shoulders and walking with her slowly toward the house as Braden dropped behind. 'I understand. It's as if Mother harbored some grudge against us that we didn't know about.' She waited until Claudia took a deep breath to bring her emotions under control.

Claudia swallowed. 'I was down on Labor Day. She was doing all right then. I would never have suspected . . . ' She gestured plaintively. Leigh nodded and waited for her to continue.

'I never suspected she had done anything about her will. I never thought about it at all.' She paused, then said, 'I know I used to think she seemed not to miss Father very much. It was like she had put some sort of distance between herself and his death.'

'The way I have now,' Leigh murmured to herself.

'What?'

She shook her head. 'Oh, nothing. It's just this odd feeling that Mother has separated herself from us by doing this.' Then she smiled sympathetically at Claudia. 'Oh, never mind. I'm sure I can't figure it out.'

She and Claudia dropped arms as they walked up the steps and entered the house. They stopped in the entry hall near the door to the living room.

'It puzzles me, though, sis,' Leigh said. 'Why did she do it? She must have had a reason.' Leigh glanced through the door at the portrait in the living room. But the eyes were not telling, and even in the oil painting, Sybil's lips were drawn shut, her message sealed.

Braden followed them in and seemed to be looking for something. 'Oh, there they are,' he said as he picked up a pair of gray leather gloves from the side table under the gilt-framed mirror.

'Oh, I'm being rude. Are you leaving, Braden?' said Leigh. She noticed how easily his name rolled off her tongue.

He was standing by the door, fumbling

with the keys in his pocket. 'Yes. But please let me know if there's anything I can do.'

Leigh nodded. Emotions tumbled over each other inside her, and she didn't really want to talk anymore. She felt tired and wanted to be alone. As if he sensed her mood, Braden opened the door.

'Goodbye then,' he said. She followed him to the porch and waved as he got into the Volvo. She stood for a while, watching him drive toward the wrought-iron gates that separated the grounds from the street.

She stared at the overhanging oaks, some of the heavy branches scraping across the top of his car as he passed under them. Then she heard the gates clang shut, and turned to go in.

When she entered the hall, Claudia had gone, but Anastasia was just coming out of the library. She glanced at Leigh, a surprised look on her face. Leigh tried to smile at her, feeling somehow uncomfortable under Anastasia's scrutinizing eye.

'Where have you been?' asked Anastasia.

'Why I just walked up to Tree Rock. You remember — ' But Anastasia cut her off.

'What were you talking about outside?'

Leigh drew in a breath. Then she gazed back at Anastasia, unflinching under the glare of her older sister's eyes.

37

'Anastasia, there's no need to snap. We were just chatting. And yes, we did mention the will. Braden, that is, Mr. Lancaster assured us there were no loopholes in it.' She sighed, trying to understand her sister's bad mood. Of course, Anastasia had always been closer to Sybil than the rest of the girls, and being cut out of the will must have felt like a particular slap in the face.

Anastasia was frowning deeply. Then she glanced up, as if just realizing Leigh was still there. She lifted her brow. 'We'll just have to let matters take their course then, won't we?'

The way she spoke sent a shiver through Leigh. She had seen Anastasia in moods like this before and knew her sister's temper.

'Anastasia, I hope you're not going to do anything rash. We're all disappointed, even if we hate to admit it. Let's give ourselves time to try to understand Mother's intentions.'

She lifted a hand to take her sister's arm in a gesture of sympathy, much as she would do with Claudia or Hania, but Anastasia stiffened, and Leigh dropped her hand to her side.

Then Anastasia seemed to try to relax and smile. 'I'm afraid I haven't your patience.' But her expression was forced. 'You're right of course. Time will tell.' Then she studied

Leigh as if gauging a reaction to her next words.

'You don't really know why then?' Anastasia asked slowly.

'Why Mother left everything to Hania? I haven't the slightest idea. It surprised me as much as you.'

'She never told you anything, even a long time ago?'

'No.' The question puzzled Leigh.

Anastasia let out the breath she'd been holding. 'Never mind. It doesn't matter.'

Leigh watched her go up the stairs, but the uneasy feeling persisted. What had Anastasia meant? She wondered if Anastasia was going to question Hania. Perhaps she would ask her to share the inheritance with the rest of them, Leigh thought as she placed her hand on the newel post. She shook her head. If Anastasia was going to beg for money, she must really be desperate.

[Journal Entry]   April 10, 1938

Played piano for Daddy tonight. I mastered
the fingering on the Sonata in E minor, and
he noticed. I didn't care for the two men
Daddy had to dinner though. They work for
him on the railroad. One was a bit nicer.
Hawthorne Castle. He has reddish hair and a
mustache, and he seemed to like my music.
But the other one, Charlie Sutter, has dark
hair and a smirk, and he isn't a gentleman. I
hope they don't come again. It's better to
play just for Daddy. He appreciates me and
my music. I don't think everyone else does.
Maybe Mama did when she was alive, but
that was a long time ago.

— S.P.

3

Mrs. Garcia had laid out the food the neighbors had brought for the family to have a buffet dinner. Leigh and Claudia were in the kitchen, uncovering the bowls and platters filled with chicken, meat loaf, noodles, and tossed salad.

'Umm,' said Claudia, dipping a finger into some custard. 'We definitely won't starve.'

For a while, Leigh was able to concentrate on the food. She and Claudia helped Mrs. Garcia rummage among the utensils for serving spoons, knives to cut a loaf of fresh bread, plates, and napkins. By keeping her hands busy, Leigh kept her mind off the events of the day.

Yet the images from the funeral floated in the background. She had only to look at the somber colors she wore or remember who had brought the food.

'You all right, sis?' Claudia's voice penetrated Leigh's consciousness. She looked up and realized she was standing over a tray of cold cuts sitting out on the kitchen table. Had she been about to take the tray to the dining room?

'Oh, yes,' she said, her hand posed selfconsciously on the plastic wrap that covered the meats. 'I must have been daydreaming.'

'It's all right,' Claudia said in a low voice, and Leigh knew she understood. She gave Claudia a half smile, then watched her bend over a plate of raw vegetables in her brisk, efficient manner. Claudia took the plate through the door and across the hall to the dining room.

Claudia, in Leigh's opinion, was the most stable of the four sisters. She had always handled problems well. Even when they were younger, she was able to take no for an answer. When they couldn't have ice cream, or when they couldn't play at the shale pit, Claudia always seemed to understand the reason why, and she would explain it to the other girls.

Of course, Hania always accepted everything too. But she was older. She accepted everything because one of their parents said it was so. Hania was the opposite of Anastasia of course. Leigh could well remember Anastasia's temper tantrums when their father refused to take the girls on another sled ride up the hill. Leigh could picture Hawthorne carrying the sled across the yard, tired but happy after the day's exertions with his daughters.

'I'm not finished,' Anastasia would say, hands on hips in her red flannel playsuit. 'I want to go one more time, please, Daddy,' she would beg, running after him.

But Hawthorne was always quick to find something else to amuse her. He would lift her up and swing her around until she would laugh with dizziness. Finally, they would all traipse around the kitchen, tracking snow everywhere. If Hania had gone with them, Hawthorne would extend a hand to her to make sure she wasn't left out of the younger girls' play.

'Oh, now, look what you girls are doing,' Sybil would say as they shed coats and boots. Hania would help the younger girls off with their coats, always trying to make things easier for their mother.

Hania and Anastasia were certainly opposites as adults. It was hard to believe they were sisters. Hard to believe any of them were sisters.

'You're not thinking of using those old plates.'

Leigh opened the door to the dining room to find Anastasia confronting Claudia across the dining room table. Claudia was looking at her with exasperation on her face. Anastasia seemed to be demonstrating the very attitude Leigh had just been associating with her. Evidently the old white plates from the kitchen cupboard were not good enough for her.

In spite of Leigh's serious thoughts, she could not suppress a laugh at the disdainful look Anastasia was giving the stack of plates Claudia had placed on the table. Anastasia fingered the pearls that had replaced the gold chains when she had changed into dark-brown velvet pants and an off-white cashmere sweater. It was comical to see her arguing over so trivial a thing as plates.

'The servants eat off those,' she was saying.

But Claudia was more than a match for her. She stood, one hand on her hip, glaring coolly across at Anastasia. Funny, thought Leigh. She had always supposed that Anastasia's affluent life style had given her poise. But since the funeral, she seemed nothing but a spoiled woman, much like the spoiled child she used to be.

Claudia wasn't losing control. She had set the table. Let no one criticize it.

'Don't be silly — the family will not mind eating off these plates,' she said. 'We've already put the Lenox china away, and I see no reason to get it out for a buffet supper.'

Leigh was surprised to observe that tears

had formed at the corners of Anastasia's eyes. But then she took a closer look. No, she was acting.

'I would feel much better if we used the china, you know,' Anastasia sniveled. 'Mother's china. Of course,' she said self-righteously, 'it's not for me to say. It's not my china.'

'They're not your kitchen plates either, Anastasia. However, you'll eat on them if you're going to join us for a snack. Here, help yourself.'

Anastasia wiped her nose with a handkerchief. 'I didn't mean to interefere with your plans, Claudia. It was just a shock.'

Anastasia's face looked like she could no longer find an appropriate emotion, having failed to win her sisters over with anger or pity. She clutched the plain white plate and then turned on Leigh.

'I see you're being rather chummy with that lawyer, that Braden Lancaster. You've got him sniffing around your heels already. I wouldn't have taken you to be so clever, Leigh.'

Blood rushed to Leigh's face at the insult. 'What do you mean, Anastasia? That's a very nasty thing to say. I've only just met him, as you know.'

Anastasia gave her a haughty look. 'Well,

you were having a cozy chat with him on the hill.'

Leigh stiffened, in spite of the fact that she knew it wasn't worth it to get angry at Anastasia. 'There was nothing cozy about it. We both felt a need for some fresh air.'

'If I remember correctly,' Claudia put in, coming to Leigh's defense, 'you were rather cozy with him yourself, Anastasia, when we all gathered in the living room for the first time.'

Leigh remembered how solicitous Anastasia had been when she had introduced him. She flashed Claudia a look of thanks.

'Well,' said Anastasia, changing her tactic, 'someone's got to get next to him if we're to do anything about this dreadful will.'

Both Leigh and Claudia looked at her silently. Finally, Claudia spoke. 'What do you mean? It is clear to me what Mother wanted to do with her estate. It's no business of ours to interfere in her decision.'

'It is our business,' Anastasia sputtered, her eyes practically giving off sparks. 'She was our mother.'

'Just as I said,' replied Claudia. 'We ought to respect her decision.'

Leigh had another thought, which she did not voice. Perhaps Hawthorne had asked Sybil to do it, for Hania was Hawthorne's favorite.

Anastasia looked from one sister to the other as if trying to decide how to win them over, but there was nothing encouraging about the way either woman returned her gaze. Then she looked down at the plate she still held in her hands. 'I'm not very hungry — I believe I'll eat later,' she said, putting the plate down and leaving the room.

Leigh and Claudia looked at each other and covered their mouths with their hands to prevent themselves from laughing out loud. It looked as if Anastasia would rather go without dinner than lower herself to eat off the kitchen plates. Then they turned their attention back to the table, for the others would be coming in soon. Just then, Nathan entered from the living room. He must have run into Anastasia on the way.

'Hello, Nathan,' said Claudia. 'We're just putting out some cold cuts and things. Here are some plates. Oh, Leigh, would you bring in some silverware? Some stainless from the kitchen drawer will be fine.'

The others gathered quietly. Hania and Nathan filled their plates, and Richard struck up a conversation with Claudia, leading her to one of the wing chairs in the living room where they could talk, their plates set on the inlaid table between them. Only Anastasia was missing. And Braden.

It was odd to find she missed him after having just met him. And it was frustrating to think that her interest in him might be exactly what Anastasia had accused her of. She felt the warmth that must be coloring her cheeks.

'What's wrong?' Claudia had left Richard and come to sit by Leigh at the end of the dining room table. She looked at Leigh with concern on her face.

Leigh smiled. 'Nothing, sis.'

'You looked angry with that chicken leg,' Claudia said.

'Oh, you know. I was just having a conversation with myself. Nothing to be concerned about.'

Claudia pulled a wry face. 'I know what you mean. We all seem to be doing that.' Then she went around the table to take another pickle.

Leigh followed her with her eyes. They were all pretty good at keeping their feelings to themselves, Leigh realized. All except Anastasia. She didn't seem to think twice about her reactions, how they made her look, much less how they affected others. Leigh shook her head and dabbed at her coleslaw. In the past she would have said that Anastasia usually concealed her true feelings. Either something about this situation had thrown her off her guard, or she just didn't care how

48

she appeared to the others.

Leigh glanced toward the living room at Claudia, who was deep in conversation with Richard again. He was nodding as she described the various facets of her job. Anastasia came in and was watching them from her position on the blue brocade sofa. She sat beside Hania, who was concentrating on her food. Anastasia made a few trivial remarks to Hania, but her attention was directed at her husband.

The look on Anastasia's face made Leigh feel suddenly uncomfortable. Why did Richard suddenly seem so interested in Claudia's job? It was almost as if he were trying to find out something. He and his wife were up to something. She could feel it. If Anastasia and Richard wanted to contest the will, they needed allies. But Braden had said that would be useless. Was there something else? Perhaps it was more subtle than looking for someone to side with them. Did Claudia know something they might be trying to find out? If so, what? She remembered her earlier conversation with Anastasia in the hall. Anastasia had questioned her about Sybil telling her something a long time ago. Was Richard now asking Claudia something along the same lines?

Leigh stood and carried her plate to the

kitchen. She must speak to Claudia — see if she agreed with her observations. Then she shook her head, chiding herself silently. She knew she felt slighted by her mother's will, and she was probably throwing suspicion around as if that would solve something, when it was her own feelings she should come to terms with first. Then she could help prevent a family squabble if there was going to be one.

But as she placed her fork and knife in the dishwasher, she remembered Braden's words. Sybil had been adamant. Whatever could have happened to make her so determined?

Braden Lancaster, Leigh almost said aloud to herself. *Mystery man. What did my mother tell your father that you can't tell her daughters?*

Outside the weeping willow brushed against the side of the house next to the kitchen window, making a strange scraping noise. Leigh shivered and turned to go back into the dining room. Then she stopped. No, why go back in there with everyone staring at everyone else, wondering what the others were thinking? It was not a pleasant environment. Wouldn't be until . . .

When? thought Leigh. Sybil had really done it, hadn't she? Set them against each other. For as open as Leigh had resolved to

50

be, she had to admit there was a tiny wedge between herself and Hania now. Had that been Sybil's intention? For what earthly purpose?

Leigh put on water for tea, just for something to do. The door opened and Claudia came in bringing trays of food, which she set on the table. 'Shall we make coffee?'

'If anyone wants it.'

'I'll do it.'

'No, I'll do it — no trouble,' said Leigh. She preferred to be here in the kitchen with Claudia than out there with the vultures. Vultures, that really did describe Anastasia and perhaps Richard too, and Hania was their prey. She shuddered at the ugly image.

'What was Richard asking you about?' Leigh asked Claudia casually, remembering her earlier notion.

Claudia shrugged. 'Wanted to know what I did and all about the firm. I never realized I knew so much about architecture until I started telling someone else. You pick up a lot at the office.'

Leigh knew her sister underrated herself. She was very capable, and Leigh knew from what Claudia had described that the principals of the firm gave her a great deal of responsibility and respected her for what she did. She was no doubt the best administrative assistant they could ever hope to find.

While Claudia bustled about with the coffee things, emptying the coffee urn of its earlier contents, Leigh expressed her concern to Claudia. She lowered her voice to a whisper so that only the two of them could hear.

'I think they're up to something,' Leigh said. 'They're looking for someone to side with them, or else they're trying to find something out.'

Claudia shook her head. 'Not me. Not even if they go through with it. Contesting the will, I mean. Did seem funny though, his taking so much interest in my work. Come to think of it, it was almost as if he were trying to ascertain how much I was worth.' She shook her head.

'Hmmm,' said Leigh. 'That's strange. I wonder.'

'What?'

'Maybe they want to make sure they're the only ones who will contest the will. It could be . . . ' But she was interrupted by the door opening and Hania coming in, several plates in her hands.

Leigh let her words hang. She hated to talk about the inheritance in front of Hania. Drat, Leigh cursed to herself. It wasn't fair that through no doing of their own, they should all feel so uncomfortable, and that the subject of the will should be so inappropriate with certain members of the family. No, it wasn't right.

Hania looked as if she knew they'd been talking about her, but she wasn't about to embarrass them. She noticed that Claudia was making coffee and approved.

'I was just going to suggest coffee,' she said as she placed the potato salad and coleslaw in the refrigerator. 'Nathan and Richard asked for it.' She said it smoothly, as if the two men were not now on opposite sides of a critical issue.

Bless Hania, Leigh thought. Always one to smooth things over, she acted as if this were a real family get-together, as if she were pleased with the duty of entertaining everyone. Well, she could afford to be hospitable. Leigh pressed her lips together, as if to stifle the words from escaping. Of course, she would never say anything like that out loud, and she reprimanded herself for even thinking it. She moved to help the other women.

After another half-hour of quiet conversation, too filled with a tense undercurrent for Leigh's taste, she decided to go for a walk. She simply could not stand to be in the house with things this way. She excused herself and went up to her room to change into jeans, a sweater and sneakers. Then she pulled on her red and black wool hunting jacket, went down the stairs to the kitchen and out the back door.

The lights from the kitchen cast their glow onto the grounds, and the moon was high, so Leigh was not in complete darkness. She stepped onto the grass that sloped gently downward toward the edge of the grounds. Between the trees, lights twinkled from the town below. The view was peaceful. She leaned against the weeping willow, whose branches brushed the side of the house.

Leigh remembered how they used to climb the tree and then get onto the roof of the house. She reached her hand up to the first toehold. She didn't remember it being so high when they were girls. But of course the tree had grown in the fifteen years since she'd climbed it.

Suddenly feeling chilled, she crossed her arms in front of her, rubbing the wool of her jacket, then turned to go back to the house. Enough for one day. Let tomorrow shed its light on the events. Perhaps things would be clearer then.

★　★　★

Leigh sat up in her bed abruptly. She could have sworn she heard something. It sounded like a door shutting above her. Then boards creaked. She was fully awake now, and she was sure of it. Someone was walking around in the attic. Leigh tossed the covers aside and put her feet on the carpet. The curtains billowed out at her. That was odd. She didn't remember opening the window. She looked at her clock. The glowing dial told her it was five minutes to three. Awfully late for someone to be prowling about. Surely it wasn't a real prowler — not in a house full of people. It was probably just another member of the family; someone who couldn't sleep. She reached for her flannel robe.

Her own door creaked as she opened it, and she winced. She peered into the hall. The rheostat on the hallway chandelier had been turned low, but not off, and it gave an eerie glow. All the bedroom doors were closed as far down the hall as she could see. Then she froze. Her heart raced, and she steadied herself with her hand on the wall.

She definitely felt a presence, as if someone were on the stairway that led up to the attic. But why would anyone go to the attic at this time of night? Least of all a prowler. He would be more interested in the family silver, to her way of thinking.

She approached the stairway. It was completely dark up to the attic, the light from the hall chandelier illuminating only the first few steps. The attic light switch was at the top of the stairs, and she had no way of knowing if there was a light bulb in the socket. She shivered. It would be silly to go exploring at this hour without a flashlight. *And*, a tiny voice said, *what if you do find someone there?*

She stood at the bottom of the stairwell and peered into the darkness. Then she called softly, 'Is anyone there?'

Silence. If one of the family was in the attic, he or she would have an explanation — and would have answered her. Anyway, the noise was probably just the old house settling, and she would disturb the others by making the stair creak even more. She decided it would be more logical to check the downstairs to see if all was secure. She only halfway admitted to herself that she didn't want to go into the dark, musty old attic alone at night.

Her heart thudding in her chest, she tiptoed down the stairs. The night light in the foyer made her breathe easier. The front doors were locked. She decided to check the windows in the library. She walked toward the large oak doors and was about to turn the handle when she looked down. A faint light shone beneath the door.

She gasped involuntarily, then tried to still her pounding heart. Someone was in the library. She pushed open the door, and Richard turned to face her, as surprised as she.

'Oh, I didn't know anyone was here,' she said, trying not to sound as startled as she felt.

'Nor I. That is, I didn't know anyone was up.' He glanced around him. 'I couldn't sleep, so I thought I might come down here and read.'

Leigh nodded. 'I heard someone, so I was just checking all the doors. The front door seems to be locked.'

'Yes, it should be,' he said, sounding rather certain.

'The windows?' she asked, then felt foolish. If the noise she had heard was Richard, then she didn't need to go snooping for a burglar.

He looked at the windows as if someone might have come in, then he walked over to them. Pulling back the heavy drapes, they could both see the windows were cranked shut and the latches were fastened.

Leigh tried to relax. 'Well, I guess everything is all right. I'll go back to bed.'

'Yes. Everything is fine.'

Turning back to the door, she stopped. Hawthorne's portrait hung above the mantel, much as Sybil's did in the living room. Why were they not in the same room? Leigh wondered. But then the idea of it struck her as daunting. It was hard enough to face one pair of eyes looking out of the canvas, as if they were still aware of the life of the household. Two pairs of eyes in the same room would be too much.

Leigh moved closer to her father's portrait. She had not really studied it in some years. The artist, one Frances Bernard, had done a very good job of capturing the man she remembered — large, alert, every hair on the beard painted in. Dominant brows, and yet a lusty twinkle in the eyes, as if he were ready to share a secret.

'Would that you could tell me that secret,' she murmured to the painting, her hands pressed on the cold mantelpiece.

Richard's eyes flicked from her face to the painting. 'A vibrant personality, no doubt,' he said.

'Yes, I was just thinking that.' She turned, rubbing her arms. 'Well, I'll say good night then.'

'Good night.'

She left him looking at the painting and started up the stairs. Back in her room, she still felt a chill and remembered her window was open. She closed it, then went back to bed.

She lay with her eyes open, pondering the old house. How many times had she lain here as a child? She thought of her mother as a younger woman, still prim and conservative. How unlike her father, Hawthorne, a big man, with a temper. Still, when he found something humorous, he had a big laugh. He would pick Leigh up and swing her high over his shoulders, making her dizzy. He was such a contrast to her mother. She remembered quieter moments with them both as well, Hania sitting with their father in front of the fireplace in the living room, the other girls sprawled on the floor around the room. Sybil seemed to have a calming effect on him at times like that.

Finally, Leigh fell into a restless sleep, dreaming of her childhood.

★   ★   ★

Leigh spent the next day going through her closet, deciding what to throw out. By dinner time she was starved. She put down the high school year-book she had been browsing through and got up from her cross-legged position to find that her right foot was asleep.

59

The tingly sensation crawled up and down her leg as she stamped her foot and limped around the room to wake it up. Then she went into the hall and down the stairs.

Passing through the front hallway, she saw Richard and Anastasia standing close together talking. As she walked by and nodded, they stopped talking, as if they didn't want her to hear what they had been saying. Anastasia smiled politely. Leigh shook her head as she went into the kitchen. That darned inheritance. It was really causing a strain in everyone.

Hania found Leigh and approached hesitantly. 'I asked Braden Lancaster to join us for dinner,' she said. Leigh looked up quickly.

'Oh?'

'I hope you don't mind.'

'No, why should I?' said Leigh, a bit too quickly.

Claudia caught part of the conversation as she came through the door with a large bowl of salad. 'I think she likes him,' she said with a wink.

'Oh, Claude,' said Leigh, using the old pet name she knew her sister hated. 'Don't be a tease.'

Claudia flicked a napkin at Leigh so that she had to duck, and soon they were laughing. Even Hania smiled, evidently glad to see them acting as they used to.

Leigh heard Braden's voice in the hallway talking to Nathan and unconsciously smoothed her hair and pulled her sweater neatly over her wool skirt.

Mrs. Garcia had prepared a hearty stew, Waldorf salad, mashed potatoes and cherry pie for dessert. Evidently she felt that leftovers from the buffet might do for lunch but what the family needed was plenty of hot food.

Anastasia remained silent during the meal. Mostly she looked at Richard, who either talked to Braden or remained sullenly silent himself.

As they came to dessert, Leigh found herself glancing often at Braden, who sat next to Hania at the end of the table. She had to force herself to concentrate on the food in front of her. Braden noticed.

'Your sister Leigh seems to be thinking hard about something,' he said to Claudia.

Leigh looked up guiltily. 'Did I miss anything?' she asked, trying to appear composed. But his deep-brown eyes fastened on hers and held them.

'No,' he said, not even trying to keep the amusement out of his voice. 'Claudia's promised to show me some family photographs later.'

Claudia nodded. Leigh smiled agreement,

then turned back to Braden. 'I thought you had business to transact.'

'Oh, just a few papers to go over. We took care of most of it at my office today. But I have some things to show Hania.' He made it seem a simple matter. If he was aware of the family tension, he did not show it. Leigh was impressed with his easy manner, but then, he said he had dealt with this sort of thing before.

When dinner was finished, Hania and Nathan went into the library with Braden. Anastasia disappeared without a word, while Leigh and Claudia saw to it that the table was cleared.

'By the way,' asked Claudia, 'how long are you staying here?'

'For a while,' said Leigh. 'There are some things I'd like to think over.'

Claudia gave Leigh a look that spoke more than words. What did Leigh have to think about? The inheritance? Something else? Someone else? Claudia was aware that Leigh's life in New York, while very busy, was impersonal in some ways. She was a glamorous translator at the UN. But glamour wasn't nurturing all the time.

'Hello,' said a baritone voice at the kitchen door. All three women looked up.

'Hello, Braden,' said Claudia. 'Are you

ready to be bored with photographs?'

'I'm ready, and I'm sure I won't be bored.' He looked at Leigh, and she didn't miss the invitation in his eyes. 'Perhaps your sister would like to see them too.'

They went to the living room, where Claudia got out the photo album stored in a drawer of the secretary. Braden adjusted a log in the fireplace, and soon a cozy glow warmed them.

Leigh had positioned herself on the end of the brocade sofa, and Braden started to seat himself next to her. Then, seeing Claudia holding the photo album, he seemed to decide at the last moment that it would be more polite to let Claudia sit in the middle.

Claudia turned the pages of the album slowly, pointing out her favorite pictures.

They paused over snapshots of themselves as teen-agers. There was one of the family at the City of Rocks. Claudia had started to turn the page, but Braden stopped her.

'What is it?' asked Leigh.

He shook his head. 'I was just noticing how like Sybil Anastasia looks in that picture.'

'Yes,' Leigh said. 'They did look alike even then.'

'Mother rather favored Anastasia, you see, perhaps because she was the prettiest one of us,' Claudia added.

He let the page turn. 'I'm not sure I would agree with that.' Leigh looked at him questioningly, but he said nothing further.

Finally, Claudia gave a yawn. 'I think I'll go to my room if you two don't mind.'

Braden stood and stretched. 'Thanks for the entertainment. This family seems to have a knack with cameras.'

'Oh, I don't know if you really enjoyed it, but we're suckers for family pictures, right, sis?'

Leigh smiled her agreement.

'I'll leave you two — good night,' said Claudia, and she put away the photo album and left.

Braden didn't seem ready to leave. He glanced at the dining room.

'Would you like a cognac?' Leigh asked. 'I wouldn't mind one myself.'

'Sounds delicious.' She crossed to the dining room and opened the china cabinet for brandy snifters. As she reached up for the glasses, she felt him move closer. She glanced at him and saw the way he eyed the curve of her breast against her Angora sweater. He lifted his eyes to hers, and she stood still, the warmth beginning deep in the center of her and spreading upward until her flesh tingled.

He did not blink but moved slowly to take the glasses out of her hands. When their fingers touched, he looked up quickly, as if he too had felt the spark that flew between them. He set the glasses down.

'Leigh,' he whispered, his hand on her arm, his face only inches from hers.

But as he leaned toward her, she turned her face slightly. He seemed to sense her hesitation and turned away.

'Sorry,' he said, the emotion in his voice telling her that he too was aroused.

'That's all right,' she said, turning back to the liquor cabinet to busy her hands. She felt highly charged emotionally but something stopped her from acknowledging her feelings for him. For one thing, the unusual circumstance of the will made her wonder if he was being completely truthful with the rest of the family. His father might know something of what had been in Sybil's mind when she changed her will, but Braden would never betray his father's confidence.

The smooth red liquid filled the two brandy snifters, then they clinked glasses and swallowed. The drink burned on its way down.

She studied Braden's features as he turned the glass in his hand, saying nothing. His eyes were lowered now, in thought, but his mouth was relaxed. As he looked up at her again, his brows lifted in question. Then from a tiny corner of her consciousness came Anastasia's nasty voice accusing her of encouraging Braden to sniff around her heels. The image broke the spell.

Of course, Anastasia's crude words were nowhere near descriptive of the emotion she felt conveyed by Braden's look, and it angered her that Anastasia had colored it so. Still, the damage was done. She turned her head to the side.

'I'm sorry,' she said, not knowing what she meant to apologize for exactly. 'It's just that we're all under a strain.'

He sighed, turning his profile to her. 'I know. And I do understand. You may not believe it, but I feel . . . involved.'

He shook his head, seeming perplexed.

'So you wonder about it too?' she asked.

He shrugged. 'Silly, isn't it. As if by pondering it or' — he gestured at the large dining room — 'staring at this house long enough, one could make it give up its secrets.'

'So you believe there are some?'

He returned his gaze to her. 'Skeletons in closets. Isn't that what they say?' Then he shook his head. 'I'm sorry. I shouldn't have said that.'

'No, that's all right.' She paused. Then she plunged on. 'My sister Anastasia thinks you know more than you're telling us.'

He paused, and she could see the veiled look that crept into his eyes. For whatever reason, he was obviously disturbed by her statement. 'I can understand why your sister would think that, but let me assure you, it's not true.'

His relaxed demeanor fled, and the professional one took over again. Leigh felt disappointed, and confused. She wanted to protect Braden from Anastasia's venom, but at the same time she had to know if there was any truth to her sister's insinuation.

She took another sip of her brandy, welcoming the fiery, fuzzy feeling it gave her. 'Well, I suppose I should go up,' she managed to get out.

'Yes,' he said, looking down. He still stood near her, an intimate distance. 'Leigh,' he said, 'perhaps you'll have dinner with me tomorrow night?'

Unsure why, she said, 'Yes, that would be nice.'

He smiled then. 'I'll pick you up at seven-thirty. We'll drive out to Los Panchos.'

She nodded. She knew the Mexican restaurant at the edge of town. He put his hand on her elbow and guided her through the living room to the foyer. In the shadowy hallway he lingered for a moment. Then gently he let her go and swung the door open.

She could just make out his shadow on the other side of the oval leaded glass as he moved down the steps from the porch.

Suddenly she was glad she had come back to Culver City, even in these gloomy times.

[Journal Entry]   **July 7, 1938**

Hawthorne Castle and Charlie Sutter were here again. After lunch I overheard them talking to Daddy about business. I don't trust them, Charlie anyway. I saw the way he looked at the maids, and later he spoke to one of them in the hallway when he thought no one was looking. I wonder if Daddy would approve of these two men if he knew they were arranging meetings with the servant girls. I know what they were talking about.

I can't tell Daddy though, for he would say it was unladylike of me to be eavesdropping.

— S.P.

4

Leigh dressed in green corduroys and an oversize cream-colored sweater for breakfast. There was a strained silence in the dining room as she went to the sideboard to help herself to scrambled eggs and bacon. She glanced at Hania, sitting with her head bowed over her plate. No one spoke to her. Leigh felt a deep sense of pity for her eldest sister. What a burden it must be to have the rest of the family resentful because of something Sybil had done. She deliberately went to sit by her. In spite of Leigh's own disappointment, she knew it wasn't Hania's fault that the other sisters had been so strangely cut out of their mother's will.

'How are you, sis?' she asked Hania.

'I'm fine,' said Hania slowly. But she looked pale. Leigh was stymied as to what to say next.

Hania lifted her head to speak. 'I think you should know something, Leigh,' she said in a sort of whisper. 'I don't think — ' she began. But just then Nathan entered from the living room.

'You don't think what, my dear?' he said.

70

He smiled convivially, but his voice betrayed his thoughts. Leigh grasped in a moment what she had suspected earlier. No matter what Hania wanted to do with the estate, Nathan was going to stop her. He most likely controlled the purse strings in their family, as he obviously controlled her. Hania's cheeks colored, and she lowered her gaze, never finishing whatever she was going to say. She must have known her husband wouldn't approve of her ideas.

Leigh decided she'd had enough for breakfast and got up to take her plate to the kitchen. As she passed through the swinging door, she found Claudia emptying the dishwasher. Carlos, the kitchen boy, was just disappearing out the back door with the garbage.

'I'll help,' said Leigh. She placed her own plate on the tile counter top and reached for a stack to put away in the cupboards above.

'Why is it funerals are almost a celebration?' Leigh asked. Then she glanced at Claudia. She didn't know how her sisters felt about their mother's death. None of them was very demonstrative except Anastasia, and her emotions were being spent on something other than grief at present.

But Claudia didn't seem to mind discussing it. 'You're right,' she sighed. 'They are, in a way, like celebrations. But then it is thoughtful of people to bring food.' She lifted her dark head to gaze out the kitchen window that overlooked the large back yard sloping down the hill. Branches of the overhanging willow moved, and an occasional leaf in the yard turned over, lifted by the wind. Thorny branches snaked their way through the latticework and rose trellises at the edge of the garden.

'It's nearly winter,' said Claudia.

Leigh moved closer and followed her sister's gaze out the window. The scene looked different than it had two nights before. It brought back many fond memories. She reached up to run her fingers across the natural-oak cabinetry above the blue-tiled counters.

'I wonder how many times we'll be together as a family after this,' she said. 'Really, we haven't been a very close family.'

'I was thinking the same thing,' said Claudia.

Leigh shook her head slowly. 'Some families are, some aren't. I suppose I didn't help any, taking off to study abroad.'

'Oh, it wasn't just you. Anastasia rarely came home, even for Christmas. She and Richard were always traveling somewhere.'

'It must have been lonely for Mother, with

only Hania and Nathan for company after Father died, and you on holidays. Maybe that's . . . ' But she didn't finish.

Claudia shrugged, catching her meaning. 'I guess so. But just because Hania married a banker and lived in town doesn't mean Mother should have favored her with the inheritance. I mean, she never objected to the rest of us going off and living our own lives. I think Nathan lost some money on investments. Still . . . '

Then she looked up, her wide brown eyes, usually full of fun, now serious as she stared into the distance. 'I felt it the other day . . . still feel it . . . sort of . . . '

'Cut off?'

Claudia nodded.

'I know. It's not the money or the house.' Leigh gestured at the tasteful surroundings. 'It's the fact that she did it willfully, as if she had a reason to set us adrift from her . . . '

'And from each other.'

Leigh paused.

Claudia shook her head. 'I wasn't all that close to her, I suppose.'

'Me either. At least I realize that now.'

Claudia lowered her voice and stepped nearer, as if the question she was about to ask was gnawing at her and had to come out. 'Do you suppose she never wanted . . . all her children?'

'I don't know,' said Leigh slowly. 'I never thought she felt that way.'

'Do you think she resented Father?'

Leigh shook her head slowly. 'You know, sis, we'll all just drive ourselves silly asking these questions.'

'And they can't be answered,' said Claudia. She sighed. 'Oh, well, I'm going to the store. Want anything?'

'No thanks.'

'OK. See you later.'

Leigh frowned. Something about the whole affair still bothered her. There was too much left unsaid. She tried to concentrate on putting away dishes, but pictures of Braden Lancaster came to mind. She wondered if he might know something after all. Or if he didn't know exactly, perhaps he knew enough to guess.

He did seem to take an unusual interest in the subject. She paused with her hand on the counter. What if he suspected that something fraudulent had been done, then covered up? Or, and this thought troubled her even more, what if his interest in her was because of the will? Perhaps he did have more to do with it than met the eye.

Leigh walked idly into the dining room and

stared at the pattern in the parquet floor. She wondered what Hania had been about to say this morning. Hania had most likely considered things and decided to make a gift to her sisters of part of the estate. It would be a generous gesture, and one Leigh was sure Hania was capable of. But Nathan would stop her. At least it appeared so.

Leigh sat down again at the empty oval table and looked at her reflection in the polished wood. Soon the family would disperse. And for how long this time? What would bring them together again? It seemed awful to see each other only at funerals.

No, she said to her reflection. It wouldn't be that way. Seeing her sisters had made her realize she was missing something. For the last four years, she had relished the cosmopolitan lifestyle in New York City, but as she grew older, her roots were beginning to pull her home. Perhaps she was looking for something; she wasn't sure what.

Thoughts of Braden Lancaster both confused and compelled her. She wanted to be sure of her reasons for seeing him, though. She couldn't deny the electricity that passed between them. But if he harbored knowledge about her family, she had to find out. She had to be sure of his motives.

★ ★ ★

Leigh sat across from Braden at a small table in an intimate corner of Los Panchos. The sound of guitar music drifted to their table and colorful *piñatas* hung from the ceiling over their heads in the shapes of donkeys, sombreros and other playful objects.

Braden looked elegant and comfortable in a smoky blue and gray herringbone sport coat, light-blue oxford-cloth shirt and gray wool tie. The colors made his face and hair look darker. Again Leigh thought he dressed a cut above the average Culver City professional. Come to think of it, he and his father must have done extremely well as attorneys here.

'More wine?' he asked, lifting the bottle in the center of the table to pour.

'Half a glass,' Leigh said, feeling a slight buzz from her earlier glass. The light silk of her blouse caressed her arms when she moved, and the crepe of her dark-pink skirt rustled as she crossed her legs. It was a relief to indulge in the pleasures of the senses, although Leigh warned herself not to become too relaxed.

She pondered the man across from her. The signals that passed between them were unmistakable, and Leigh realized she needed to control their flirtation, which would only lead them into trouble if it continued. She had a reason for seeing him, and she mustn't forget it.

They had eaten slowly, talked softly. Neither seemed to be in a hurry to end the evening. She had told him about living in Rome, then about her job at the UN, and he had answered her questions about going to law school in Washington, then returning home to go into practice with his dad.

They had agreed that there were certain things to be gained from living in a small town. And the clean air and open spaces of the desert, with the cool mountains rising around the little town, appealed to them more now that they had each seen some of the world.

When she wrinkled a brow, Braden noticed and said, 'A penny for your thoughts.'

She laughed. 'I'm not sure they're worth that much.'

He tilted his head and looked at her questioningly. 'I'll be the judge of that.'

She became more serious and turned her wine glass by the stem with her fingers as she pondered her answer. 'I was just thinking about the future.'

'Is New York home now?'

'That's just it. I'm not sure.' She felt him

watching her, and she grew embarrassed. It sounded like she was angling for a proposition. He cleared his throat as if he wanted to say something.

Even though the lighting was dim, cast only by the pin lights overhead and the flickering candle between them, she could see the intent look in his eyes. She could tell he was attracted to her, but there was something else there too; something was making him hesitate.

'What is it?' she asked. She gave him a questioning look. Then it came over her again that they were not just two people attracted to one another, but a mother's daughter and the mother's lawyer, and the events that had brought them together also created a gulf between them. For some reason, a mental picture of her mother's casket being lowered into the ground flashed into Leigh's mind. She frowned deeply. She had the notion that with the casket went a secret she would never know.

Braden moved to refill her drink. He took a sip and swallowed before he spoke. 'What were you thinking?'

Her mind was fuzzy from the wine, and his nearness warmed her, but her sensations were clouded with the somber picture of the casket going into the grave. Then she remembered something else. Braden had been frowning at the casket, contemplating it in a puzzling manner himself that day.

'Braden, you remember the funeral? The burial, that is.'

He leaned back, out of the candle light. 'Of course, unfortunately. Or maybe not so unfortunately.' He gave her a slow smile, his lips tilting slightly and his eyes luminescent, even in the shadows. A more serious look replaced the grin. 'Unfortunately because your mother passed away.' He paused. 'Fortunately because I met her daughter.'

His compliment warmed her, but she was still aware of many unanswered questions. 'You looked thoughtful that day,' she said. 'I remember the black look you gave as the casket was being lowered.'

'I didn't know you were so attentive.'

'You're trying to make me blush. But I did wonder about that look. As if you were angry at Sybil for dying.'

'Well, not dying, exactly.' His serious look was replaced by something Leigh could not quite name as he placed his linen napkin on the table.

'Oh?' she said. 'The will.' It was a statement, not a question.

'Yes.'

'You knew what was in it.'

'Yes.'

'But why did you seem so displeased? You really didn't know any of us. Why should it matter how your client dispensed her fortune?'

'You forget,' he said with a gesture she had come to recognize as a professional mannerism, 'I had met you all the day before.'

'And your heart went out to the three pitiful little sisters who would be bereft.' She said it with irony, but then was afraid it sounded petty.

He grimaced. 'None of you looked very pitiful.'

Leigh gave a short laugh. 'Especially the vivacious Anastasia. She hardly looked bereft, I'm sure.' It was no use pretending. Her feelings were beginning to surface. She was suddenly driven to know the reasons behind everyone's behavior.

Braden shrugged, his thoughts now turned to the Hazletts as well. 'She and her husband dress well, and they travel abroad, but that doesn't mean anything. You don't know what sort of money they're living on, where it came from, do you?'

'No,' said Leigh. 'And they seemed more upset at being cut out of the will than the rest of us. As if they had more reason to be. But then Anastasia's behavior has never been very predictable. I wonder if she and Richard have lived above their means and were counting on part of the inheritance.'

'Something like that.'

'You mean they might have serious debts or . . .'

'Who knows? It could be anything.' He sighed. 'But no matter. It doesn't help with the matter at hand.'

'Why Sybil wrote her will the way she did.'

He stared hard at her. 'That's right.'

She still wondered if he knew more than he was telling. The doubt inserted itself, dissolving the intimacy Leigh had felt a moment ago. She shifted uncomfortably.

As if sensing her thoughts, Braden signaled for coffee, and they waited to speak until the waiter had left.

'I hope your mother's being my client doesn't color your feelings for me, Leigh. I've come to like you very much.'

His words invaded her heart and pushed at the menace of her mother's death and the troublesome will.

'Tell me,' she began, then stopped.

'What?'

She knew if she were to get to know Braden Lancaster, she had to settle her doubts about his part in her mother's will first. She plunged ahead with her questions.

'Tell me about your firm. It's just the two of you?'

'It is now.'

'Did you know Gregory Tyson?'

Braden shook his head, and Leigh became aware of what sounded like the third degree. 'Oh, I didn't mean to sound so . . . .'

'Suspicious?'

'Well . . . just a little nosy.'

Braden fingered his coffee cup. 'You're not really suspicious, I hope.'

'Oh . . . ' She had not meant for the conversation to go this way. Braden was studying her, and his somber gaze, after the rapport that was beginning to develop between them, bothered her. It was as if he were gauging her reactions. Then she realized she hadn't answered his question.

'No, no,' she managed to get out. 'I've no reason to be suspicious, have I?'

'I'm sure I don't know,' he said, returning to the coffee.

'What do you mean?' Now she was feeling paranoid, reading something into everything he said. 'You swore the will was legitimate. I know you wouldn't lie about a thing like that. Would you?'

He shook his head. 'Of course not. But that doesn't explain why she did it.'

Leigh frowned. 'I'm trying to forget about

that. We can never know why she did it, and it's not going to cause a family feud if I can help it. No one's going to do anything about it unless . . . ' She looked up to meet his gaze and saw that his dark-brown eyes were extremely intent and alert.

'Anastasia,' he finished.

She nodded, then shook herself. A shiver had run over her, and she didn't know why. 'Of course.'

'Yes,' he said, lowering his left eyebrow into a frown. 'They came to see me.'

She wondered why he hadn't said as much earlier. 'What did they . . . oh, I don't suppose you can tell me.'

'Why not? I don't represent them, so I have no confidential relationship with them.'

'Like you did with Mother.'

'That's right. Even though my relationship with her was a belated one. In fact, I only knew her to say hello. It was obvious to my father that she preferred Gregory Tyson to anyone else. Even with my father, she was cool, distant. Tyson was her lawyer before he and my father met.'

Then Leigh had another thought as she sipped her coffee slowly. Supposing there was something Sybil had told him under that confidentiality that Braden wanted Leigh to know, but couldn't tell her. If there was a way

83

for her to find out on her own, he would surely not stand in her way. She put her coffee cup down with a clatter, causing Braden to look at her.

'What is it?' he asked.

'I just — ' she began, then tilted her head, focusing beyond him. 'I just realized that the implications may be greater than I thought.'

'How so?' He leaned closer. Was that a look of encouragement she saw in his eyes?

She shook her head. 'I don't know yet. But I just got a feeling about the situation that I hadn't had before. I guess you might call it a premonition.'

'Go on.'

'Well, when Mother first died, I guess I was so caught up in that, and the strangeness of being back home again, I really didn't think about inheriting anything. Then when you read the will, I was, of course, shocked. Everyone was. But it really didn't affect me personally, that is until . . . ' Her voice trailed off as she remembered the scene the way it had occurred.

Anastasia had jumped to her feet. Richard had started talking immediately. It wasn't for a few minutes, Leigh recalled, that she had turned to look at Hania. Claudia had been staring at her as if she were waiting for Hania to speak. But Hania had said nothing.

Neither had Nathan. Come to think of it, that was rather strange. Leigh sighed as the vision faded. What was so peculiar about it? Honest reactions all around . . .

'You seem a thousand miles away,' Braden said.

She brought her thoughts back to the present and laughed. 'No, only a mile.'

It took him a moment to realize she meant the distance between the restaurant and her family's home. Then the light flickered in his eyes.

'Oh, I see. You mean you were recalling the reading of the will.'

Her lightheartedness faded, and she said, 'Yes, I was. But whatever bothered me about it is lost.' She gave Braden a half smile as he reached across the table for her hand.

'Let's forget about all this for now.'

After dinner they walked slowly from the restaurant to the car. Stars gleamed overhead, and Braden held her arm. She felt drawn toward him, feeling his strength. He unlocked the car door and helped her in. She was acutely aware of the smell of leather and upholstery mixed with the tang of Braden's aftershave. Being with him heightened her senses.

Just as they entered the city limits, he asked, 'Care for a nightcap at my place? We could listen to some of my Beethoven collection.'

She hesitated. She really didn't want to go home yet. She also realized that she wanted to know Braden better.

'That sounds fine.' She wondered if she had spoken too quickly. But Braden seemed pleased, so she allowed herself to enjoy the spontaneity of the occasion.

The Lancaster home was in a new development on the north side of town, near the top of a hill where the street ended in a wide cul-de-sac. The cream-colored brick structure sprawled over the edge of the hill to the side and back. The low-lying structure with its mission tile roof was a perfect example of Spanish-style architecture, with archways over the entrances and windows.

Braden pulled the car into the circular drive and got out. Then he came around to help Leigh out of the car. She followed him up the flagstone walk to the circular steps that led to an arched brick entry.

Inside, a small lamp on a table in the foyer cast a dim glow in the front part of the house. Stepping down into the sunken living room, she saw that another glow came from a small stained-glass lamp in the far corner, making the large living room with its beamed cathedral ceiling seem warm and cozy.

'How lovely,' she said. Dark, intricately carved Spanish-style furniture was accented here and there by Navaho rugs and wall hangings. Braden had come up behind her and put his hand on her waist. She relaxed against him, feeling mellow after wine and the dinner.

'Hmmm,' he said, smelling her hair. 'I like your perfume. Smells like gardenias.'

'Thank you.'

He led her across to the sofa situated approximately in the center of the room facing a circular stone fireplace, then he walked over to a large chestnut cabinet built into the far end of the living room. He opened the cabinet to reveal a stereo system and an extensive record collection. He leafed through the albums until he found what he wanted.

'*The Leonora Overtures.*'

'A good choice.' Leigh knew the opera, *Fidelio*, and the fact that Beethoven had written four overtures for it.

Braden set the record on the turntable, and soon the melodious music surrounded Leigh as she leaned back on the sofa. Braden crossed to the fireplace directly in front of her. Taking off his jacket, he knelt to light some tinder, waiting until the flames licked the two heavy logs set in the fireplace.

When the fire was started, he went to the liquor cabinet next to the stereo. Leigh was about to refuse another drink, but when she saw him pour only a small amount of cognac into two glasses, she decided she would have just a taste.

He handed her the glass and raised his in a salute as he sat down next to her. The liquid was sweet on her tongue. She leaned forward to put her glass on the wooden coffee table in front of her, and as she did so, she felt Braden's fingers on the back of her neck.

'Leigh,' he said.

She leaned back. 'Yes?'

He parted his lips as if to answer, but then the look in his eyes changed, and he was drawn to kiss her instead. When their lips met, she felt his arms go around her and pull her closer to him until she could feel the beating of his heart against her breast.

Even the woolly herringbone she had smelled when she had first leaned against him at the door seemed filled with his own individual scent and the lemon-lime of his aftershave.

'Leigh,' he said again softly, moving his lips from her face to her ear. His hands gripped her tighter, and she felt a tremor run through her. She made a small sound in her throat, and Braden pulled back to look at her face.

'Am I moving too fast?' he asked. His dark eyes gleamed, reflecting the firelight.

'No, I, that is . . . ' Leigh trailed off. It was hard to explain her feelings. She had met more aggressive men before, but Braden's question had a certain intensity about it that bothered her.

But then she was swept away with the feel of him, and she answered his question with a kiss, her arms tightening around him. His kiss deepened, and his hand brushed across her breast. She slipped her arms higher around him and let him caress her again.

His breathing quickened, and Leigh suddenly realized how much she wanted this man. She knew that if they were to stop, the time was now, when she could still conjure up the words to push him away from her, but suddenly the depression of the last few days and the drain on her emotions cried out for release. He was filling her up with a new kind of energy, born of caring and culminating in desire.

Yes, her body cried, and her mind agreed. So what if they had only known each other for three days. So what if there had been a death in the family recently. At this moment she did not care that their passion had no real commitment attached to it. She wanted to experience the fulfillment of the desire and heady sensation that was taking over every inch of her body.

Braden's hair fell over his brow, but even in the firelight, Leigh could see the intensity of the desire in his eyes. His lips were parted and his eyes were dark pools. He stood suddenly and, helping her up, led her through a hallway, down a few steps to the bedroom. She stepped inside, and he closed the door. Leigh gave herself a moment to adjust to the dark. Then, making out the shape of a king-size bed in the middle of the room, she walked toward it. Braden joined her, quickly unbuttoning his shirt and unknotting his tie. From the moonlight streaming through the open window, she could see his lithe form as he undressed.

Instinctively she reached for him as he took two steps toward her and gently disrobed her. 'You're beautiful,' he murmured, running one finger down along her chin and throat, over the curve of her right breast to her waist and thigh.

He lowered her to the bed, and Leigh abandoned herself to the melting sensations of love-making, giving and taking pleasure as she explored him and responded to his caresses. His lips were warm and firm, his hands gentle as they moved over her.

They sought each other in the darkness,

and he groaned in pleasure as she let her hands play over every part of him. Finally he rolled on top of her, his fingers preparing her for his possession of her. With a deep sigh he entered her.

Leigh clutched his shoulders and threw her head back as she moved toward him and away, letting him create the rhythm that took them to a new height of pleasure. Then their passion exploded fiercely, the release intense.

At last they lay together in the darkness. She raised up on her elbow, smiling at him, her breast lying against his shoulder. He was spent, but the joy in her heart would keep her awake awhile longer. She studied his profile in the moonlight. The face had strong proportions, set off only slightly by that impish, slightly crooked mouth. She watched him breathe.

5

The warm water sloshed over Leigh's tawny hair and washed the lather down over her body, trickling between her toes, over the pink and green tiles, and down the drain. She hummed to herself as she let pleasant images float in and out of her mind. The sun had shone in the window, waking them. She felt happy, having squelched the doubts of the day before. She knew she wanted to continue seeing Braden, and she hoped he felt the same way.

She was not in the habit of going to bed with a man on the first date. She realized that their emotional outpouring the night before was partially the result of pent-up nerves. They had not spoken in the car when he brought her home. But whenever he could let go of the steering wheel, he had reached over and gently touched her. The memory was warm and pleasant — the first happy thought she'd had since she'd been home.

She stepped out of the shower and reached for an oversize blue terry-cloth bath towel. Then she spied some talcum powder on the shelf above the sink and dabbed a bit on her skin.

She was just coming downstairs when she heard the phone ring. Claudia came into the hall. 'It's for you. Braden.'

Leigh hurried down and picked up the hall phone. She heard the click as Claudia hung up the extension in the library.

After they had said good morning, Braden suggested, 'How 'bout taking a drive today?'

'Don't you have to work?'

'It's Saturday.'

'Oh, so it is. I guess I've lost track of the days.'

'Then let's go. I hope you've got on some outdoor clothes.'

'I'll have to change.' She blushed in spite of herself. She wondered if her family would criticize her for spending so much time with him. But there was really no reason to stay at the house today, so she accepted the invitation.

★   ★   ★

After filling up with gas and stopping to buy picnic supplies, Leigh and Braden drove his Wagoneer up Highway 15 toward the Gila Wilderness. He'd bought the Wagoneer for trips to the mountains, since he and his dad both liked to camp and fish.

'It releases the tension,' he said as they wound up the hairpin curves leading away from the little town, farther into the mountains of the Black Range. Here the towering pines and softly babbling brooks lured those in need of serenity.

'I wouldn't think working in Culver City would have much tension connected to it,' she said.

'It doesn't ordinarily.'

She nodded in acknowledgment. She knew he must be referring to cases such as the present one. She looked now at the rolling terrain; the forest that hugged the mountains on either side, the rushing stream that peeked out from between the trees every so often. She'd been born in this part of the country, and it would always be a part of her. She realized that although she had needed to get away from it as a young person, she could very well learn to love living here again.

This had been Apache country until the late 1800s, when the elusive Geronimo finally surrendered to U.S. troops. White farmers had turned the Indians against them and left a legacy of violence. Of course the Apaches weren't the first people to call the Gila Wilderness their own. Four hundred years before Europeans ever set foot in the area, the

Mogollon Indians had made homes in spacious caves such as those they were going to visit today. Then, by A.D. 1350, for some reason unknown to archaeologists of later times — perhaps drought, overuse of resources, or war — these people had disappeared from the area. They left no clue as to where they'd gone.

Braden settled the Wagoneer in the parking area off the road, at the bottom of the trail leading to the Gila Cliff Dwellings. Several other cars indicated there must be picnickers or hikers nearby.

'Look,' said Leigh. 'Isn't that the Lincoln Anastasia and Richard drove from El Paso?'

Braden looked at the car she pointed to. 'It does look like the one I saw in your drive. Are you sure?'

She shook her head. 'It couldn't be. Since when did those two go for outdoor hikes?'

Leigh got out of the car and bent down to tie her shoelaces. Before they'd left the house, she had told Hania where she and Braden were going, promising to be back in time for supper.

'Don't hurry,' Hania had said, seeing her to the porch. 'I'm glad you're getting out.'

She had squeezed Hania's arm and then, glancing up, had caught Anastasia watching them from the living room windows. Had it been Leigh's imagination, she wondered, or did Anastasia seem troubled by the fact that her two sisters were talking? Anastasia's eyes were narrowed and her expression hateful. Leigh only remembered the incident now as she climbed the steps leading to a bridge over a stream at the bottom of the trail.

Leigh had been on this trail about twelve years ago and knew the path was steep. She walked slowly behind Braden.

'I wonder why they left,' he said.

'The Cliff Dwellers?' asked Leigh. 'I don't know.' They walked near a small stream that formed a canyon and stopped to follow the trickling water with their eyes. 'You can see why this was a good place to live,' she said. 'The stream must have supplied water year around.'

'And they would have eaten the plants and animals that depended on the stream as well.'

They walked on in silence, and Leigh tried to imagine the environment as the Cliff Dwellers experienced it long ago. To the right and left of them, ponderosa and piñon pine clung to the canyon floor as it rose to the jagged outcroppings of rock, worn smooth in places by time. Dark stains of desert varnish ran down some of the layers of rock. Here, the people hunted for turkey, deer, elk, or rabbits to take to their homes far above.

Sunlight flickered through the trees, and Leigh began to feel warm in spite of the cool air. She paused to unbutton the red hunting jacket she wore.

'Look,' said Braden, pointing above them. They could see seven natural caves in the southeast-facing cliff of the canyon, about 150 feet above them. Other tourists were making their way from one cave to the next.

'Ah, yes,' said Leigh, shading her eyes with her hand.

'How would you like to live there?'

'Well, I'd get my exercise getting up there.' She laughed. It felt good.

'Forty or fifty people lived in those caves,' said Braden.

'Odd, isn't it, that they're gone now.'

'Not so odd. That was over six hundred years ago.'

A chill passed through her as she shook her head. 'The passing of time.'

Braden nodded, but his gaze was focused on the people above them. Leigh glanced at him and saw him frown, then shake his head. He turned to her.

'Come on,' he said, reaching for her hand. 'We'll never get to the top if we stay here staring up at it.'

She returned his look, her eyes reflecting the warmth she saw in his now. 'You're right.

I promise not to distract you further from your objective.'

He looked at her oddly for a moment. 'Yes,' he said.

Leigh was about to ask him why the strange expression when it passed, and the crooked smile took its place. She decided she'd probably imagined it. Besides, she couldn't be grilling him on his private thoughts all the time. He would share things with her when he wished to.

Leigh was so engrossed in her thoughts that she failed to notice the sky darken above them. A sudden chill pervaded the air, and Leigh shivered as she looked up, pulling her jacket around her again. Just then a few drops of rain splattered on her face, and she heard Braden give a groan.

'Wouldn't you know it,' he said. 'We're not far from the caves. If we hurry, we can take shelter there.'

Leigh nodded, and they picked up their pace. In a little more than five minutes they arrived at the first cave and stepped inside. Of the three storage rooms that had once stood there, all that remained were the foundations. Leigh looked down at the fire pit for cooking and the two pot rests for large, round-bottomed jars.

A flash of lightning followed by a loud clap

of thunder surprised Leigh, and she jumped. Braden steadied her with an arm around her shoulders. 'Better come on in here,' he said. 'Keep dry.'

He led her deeper into the cave, and with the darkness outside and the rain coming down, the cave suddenly appeared gloomy indeed. Leigh huddled closer to Braden and shivered in spite of the nearness of his body.

'I did-didn't know it was going to rain today,' she said, her teeth chattering suddenly.

'Nor I,' said Braden gruffly. 'My oversight. I should have listened to the weather report. Especially since I was planning a hike.'

'It's not your fault,' she said. 'It rains all the time in the mountains. It'll pass soon.' Another crack of thunder sent her burrowing into his shoulder, while he reached around her with his other hand. The rain was pouring down now in a solid sheet outside the lip of the cave. But Leigh wasn't afraid of a storm. They were dry, if a bit cold, and the storm would soon pass.

Of course the canyon might flood. But that was a silly thought. It would take hours of torrential downpour to flood the stream, and this rain would probably not last the hour.

Still, there were places on the trail that might be washed out if it did rain for very long. Flash floods could build to destructive

99

power in just a few hours, she knew.

She moved her face slightly so as to see Braden's face. He was staring straight ahead, glaring into the rain. His look did little to reassure her. Perhaps he was concerned about the same things. Then he turned to her.

'Warmer now?' he asked.

'Uh, huh.' She nodded, beginning to get her courage back.

The rain continued to pour down outside their cave, clattering on the rocks. Leigh reminded herself that it must have rained here often in the Mogollons' time. If she peered through the curtain of rain outside, she could almost see the small dark-skinned people, slight of build, yet muscular. She could imagine the women wearing small cotton blankets around their shoulders, skirts of yucca cord, and sandals plaited of yucca, agave leaves, and bark. The men wore woven cotton breechclouts, blankets of turkey feathers, and animal skins for warmth. Leigh wished she had a turkey-feather blanket now to keep her warm.

Then she froze. From somewhere on the other side of the cave wall she distinctly heard a loud moan, as if someone were imprisoned within. The hair on the back of her neck stood on end, and she went rigid.

'Did you hear that?' she whispered.

But from Braden's stiff posture she knew the answer even before he spoke. 'Probably just the wind,' he said.

Of course. It had to be the wind. What else could it be? Wind echoing in the deep caves would be bound to create such noises. There had been tourists on the trail above them, but they had probably made it down before the storm began. And people hadn't inhabited these caves in six hundred years. Leigh became aware that she was trembling from head to foot.

She clutched Braden's arm convulsively as the next thought came to her. What if there was someone in the next cave, and what if he or she were hurt?

Braden seemed to harbor similar thoughts, for he turned in the direction the moan came from and peered at the cave wall. Solid rock. But supposing the sound was carried by the wind from one of the other caves. Given the eerie accoustics of the place, that was possible, and there might be an opening.

Braden gripped her arm. 'Listen, do you hear it?'

The rain had been pelting down so hard that she failed to hear it at first. Then, there it was again, a low moaning sound.

'I've got to go find out what it is,' said Braden, extricating himself from Leigh.

'No, Braden, don't.'

He leaned over, loosening her hands from his arm. 'Don't be frightened. I'll be right back. That sound is unnerving, and I'm sure we'll both feel better once I locate its source.'

Leigh knew this was probably true, but being left alone seemed worse. She let go of him, however, and made an effort to still her pounding heart. The storm was frightening her, that was all. And Braden was right. The sound came again, and though she had almost grown used to it, Leigh realized the sooner they located the cause of it, the sooner they could relax and wait out the storm. It was probably just the wind, but if it was someone who had been hurt, they should know. Or perhaps an animal had been trapped in a crevice and couldn't get out. She shuddered at this last possibility, for an animal in pain could be vicious.

'Be careful,' she said as he walked over the loose rocks toward the opening of the cave. He'll get drenched, she realized, for they hadn't brought slickers.

Suddenly, Braden disappeared behind the curtain of rain, leaving Leigh alone in the cave. Thunder crashed again, and she flung herself back against the ancient walls. It seemed so dark, yet she knew it must be early afternoon.

She listened, trying to hear any sounds. But all she could make out was the clatter of rain on the rocks and pebbles outside. Becoming impatient, she crept nearer to the entrance, crouching on her heels to see if she could see anything. She tried to remember what lay in the caves farther on, hoping Braden would be careful and not climb or lean on walls that were marked as dangerous areas.

After a while the rain seemed to let up a little, and Leigh put her hand out. Feeling only a slight wetness, she decided to go in search of Braden.

She turned up the collar of her hunting jacket and ventured out onto the trail. It was still raining, but lighter now, and the thunder was more distant. Still, the rocks were slick, and she would have to watch her step.

Where had Braden gone? She didn't see him anywhere, even though she could now see the mouths of the other caves. They gaped out of the side of the cliff, and a narrow path led from one to the other. She glanced down the path at places very near the edge, where excess water had created mud.

Leigh carefully made her way along. 'Braden?' she called out.

No answer. That was odd. Where could he be? There was not a great distance from here to the last cave, and even if he was in one of the small rooms of the habitations, surely he would be able to hear her. A shudder of fear ran through her. Surely he would be back for her.

She passed in and out of the caves. One room had never been completed. The floor had never been leveled as in the other rooms. On the outside corner of its nearest wall, some thin stones protruded, probably joining stones for an intended addition to the village. She went on, passing a dwelling that must have been two stories tall, judging from the frames and the two doorways. Smoke holes above the doors would have allowed for ventilation.

The sky was lighter now, dispelling some of the gloom the storm had brought. She made her way between rooms, passing a large storage bin. She stopped in front of some Indian pictographs drawn with red hematite, briefly pondering the meaning of the drawings. Glancing up, she saw the black coating of soot left by smoke from fires, the immediacy of the long-ago past chilling her again. She could imagine the men conducting their prayers and rituals. She could almost hear their laughter and voices.

Then she jerked herself up as she heard rocks sliding outside like pebbles moving under a footstep. Braden must be coming back up the trail. She made her way outside and found herself near a ladder leading down to the main trail out of the canyon.

'Braden,' she called out.

'Braden, Braden,' answered her echo. She waited, but he didn't call back. She looked at the ladder. Should she take it? If Braden was coming up the trail, then she would meet him. But why didn't he respond? She tried again. Still no answer, only her own disembodied voice bouncing off the canyon walls.

The rain had stopped completely now, leaving only the refreshing smell of dampness behind. She shook her head, remembering how frightened she had been before. It was just a storm after all.

Reasoning that Braden must have gone farther down the trail, she decided to take the ladder. Perhaps he had indeed found someone who had been injured and was leading him out — or even a small animal that needed nursing. In any case, she felt calmer now and knew that once out of the canyon, she would probably meet Braden at the car. She walked to the ladder.

For a moment, dizziness seized her as she looked straight down the cliff at a seventy-degree angle. But the ladder seemed firmly mounted, and she reasoned that hundreds of tourists must have climbed down it before her.

She turned around and put her foot on the top rung, clutching the top of the ladder to steady herself. In spite of the reassurances she had given herself, she was a little frightened of the height, being alone. Just then a gust of wind caught her, and she swayed slightly with the ladder. She tightened her hold and, moving her feet carefully, lowered herself, rung by rung.

She was about halfway down the ladder when she heard it. The moaning sound came from above her now, softly at first, then gathering in volume and intensity until it was almost a wail. The sound was unearthly. Was it the same sound they had heard before? This moaning sounded longer, more drawn out.

For a moment, it paralyzed her. Then she realized she had to get down and out of this place. Trembling, she put one foot after the other on the rungs of the ladder until finally she felt solid ground under her. Still the moaning sound continued, and she put her hands to her ears.

Without thinking what she was doing, she began to run. Heedless of the steep drop-off beside her or the mud sloshing at her feet, she hurried as quickly as she could. A kind of cold terror propelled her, and she imagined small brown-skinned men and women running after her, hurtling sticks and stones.

She ran on, feeling the spines of a cactus plant that caught on her jeans. She rounded the corner of a hill, and then she screamed. Braden lay sprawled face down on the ground. It looked as if his foot had caught on a dead tree's gnarled trunk and sent him sprawling. He didn't move. She felt as though her heart had stopped beating as she made her way carefully around the tree toward him. Just as she reached him, he gave a grunt and tried to roll over.

'Braden, what happened?' she said, relief sweeping through her to see him move. She knelt beside him and gingerly felt along his rib cage, then his arms, shoulders, and neck. Nothing seemed to be broken.

'Oh,' he groaned, grimacing as he turned his face toward her. She brushed away moss and leaves that clung to him, gasping at the sight of blood on his forehead.

She felt his head. A huge bump had formed over his left temple, and it was swelling. 'No, don't sit up yet,' she said, pressing him back down as he tried to maneuver himself into a sitting position.

He blinked his eyes, and it took a minute for him to focus. Then his head seemed to clear. 'It's not raining,' he said.

She smiled in relief. 'No, it quit some time ago. You gave me quite a scare though. You . . . and other things.' She stopped smiling. 'Did you see anything?'

He shook his head, raising a hand to his temple, wincing as he touched the lump forming there.

'I thought I saw someone limping along the trail ahead of me, but it was raining so hard I couldn't be sure.'

'Do you think you can stand?' she asked. 'We've got to get something on that. We're almost down. I can drive you to the visitors center, where the ranger can treat you.'

She helped him get up, then they carefully picked their way down. The river rushed beside them, fuller now because of the rain. They concentrated on getting to the Wagoneer, not speaking. She helped him in, then went around to the driver's side. She turned on the motor and backed up to swing around toward the visitors center. The other cars that had been in the parking lot were now gone.

In a few minutes they pulled up at the park's visitors center. Braden looked toward the entrance.

'I feel all right, Leigh. I don't think we need to go in there.'

'Nonsense. That bump looks wicked. You need first aid,' she insisted.

The ranger on duty inside, a burly blond man, took one look at Braden's swollen temple and made him lie down on a cot in the small room set up for such emergencies. The ranger cleaned the cut and applied a salve. Then he gave Braden an ice pack for the swelling.

'Just rest for a few minutes,' said the ranger. 'Then Miss Castle can drive you to a doctor.'

'Doctor,' protested Braden, trying to sit up again. 'I don't need to see a doctor.'

'Hold that ice pack where I put it,' instructed the ranger, holding Braden down with a brawny arm. 'There might be a slight concussion, and your doctor should see you.'

'He's right,' said Leigh, who had watched the ministrations. 'I'll drive back to town. Is Dr. Thomas still practicing?'

Braden grumbled that he was, though he hadn't had to see the kindly old general practitioner for five years.

'How did this happen?' asked the ranger, who was concerned about the safety of the trail.

'A case of nerves,' said Braden. 'I was following a ghost.' He grimaced.

'When I found him, he was sprawled over that dead tree near the bottom.'

'I've been worried about that tree,' said the

ranger, scratching his head. 'I argue to have it removed, but the naturalists say it's an important part of the ecology of the area. Small animals live in and under it.'

'I suppose it will eventually decay into the soil,' Leigh said. 'But it's dangerous if someone doesn't see it from the bend in the trail.'

She sat on the edge of the cot, where Braden was frowning at being an invalid even for fifteen minutes. 'Who did you see on the trail?' she asked.

He moved his head slowly from side to side. 'I don't know. It looked like a woman, bent over and limping, but she was too far ahead for me to be sure. And the rain was blinding. I thought she must be hurt, and I was going to help her down the trail or back into one of the caves. But I lost sight of her. Then I wasn't certain I'd seen anything at all.' He frowned as if he could not quite explain his actions to himself.

But Leigh thought she understood. That eerie moaning had been almost hypnotic. Whether it was the cry of an injured person or the wind or something else, she didn't know, but Braden had been determined to locate it.

'Just like a man,' she teased. 'Rushing headlong into danger just to confront the source face to face.' She could see that the

110

storm and the place had brought out something primitive in him, just as it had sent chills up her spine and caused her to imagine things.

She laughed softly to herself, now that the danger was over. Surely it had been the unusual circumstances. He wouldn't have brought her up to the cliff dwellings if he'd known it was going to rain, and on a bright sunny day the echoes of the past were probably not so evident. And surely he would never have left her alone on purpose, knowing she would be so scared.

She thought again of the ceremonial room with the sooty black ceiling and imagined the figures of men and women dancing.

A tiny thought edged into her mind. Had someone meant to frighten them? Someone vindictive about Braden's part in her mother's will? She shivered at the idea. It couldn't be. After all, no one knew where they were going. No one except Hania, thought Leigh, as she remembered her conversation with her sister on the porch before they'd left.

Besides, Braden had said he was innocent of playing any part in Sybil's decision to leave her estate to Hania, and Leigh believed him. So why would anyone have a reason to make trouble for him over it now?

[Journal Entry]   **January 5, 1939**

I finally learned why Hawthorne Castle comes to see my father so often. I was stunned today when we sat in the music room, and he asked me to marry him. I could not respond.

I had not planned to marry, ever. Why should I? I am happy here, and Father needs me to look after him since Mother died. Hawthorne said he told Daddy he wanted to marry me, and Daddy approved.

I choked down my tears in front of him. I couldn't believe my daddy wants me to marry anyone. I didn't go down to dinner. I'll wait in my room until Daddy comes to see me and asks what's wrong with me. Then I'll tell him I don't want to leave him. I don't want to marry.

— S.P.

112

6

Leigh sat in the waiting room of the small office as Dr. Thomas examined Braden. She glanced at a few magazines but mostly watched out the street-level window, too distracted to read. Traffic on the wide street was fairly brisk, since this was the main thoroughfare in the town leading to Highway 90.

How sedate the town looked — a contrast to New York and to Rome, the cities that had given her the excitement and sophistication she had yearned for as a Culver City adolescent. In her teens, Culver City had been entirely too provincial for her taste. She imagined it had been the same for her other sisters.

Certainly, Anastasia had fled Culver City as soon as she could. She had moved to Sante Fe and gotten a job; then she had gone to California, where she met and married Richard Hazlett. They had traveled all over the world.

Leigh wondered if Anastasia had found what she had been looking for. She had never bothered to finish her education but managed to pick up all the social graces. Anastasia had always run with an older, faster crowd, even when they were growing up. And she wore the best clothes and had that sleek bearing that spoke of money and the best of everything. Surely she and Richard felt out of place in Culver City. They were used to wielding power in high places, but here their power didn't count.

She shook her head, the magazine lying unopened in her lap. Claudia had only gone as far away from home as Albuquerque, but she too had traveled to Europe, visiting Leigh once in Rome. And so they had scattered. All except Hania, who had married one of the town's solid citizens and been content to stay here. Quiet, demure Hania, always keeping to herself. Could that be why Sybil had left the estate to her — because her other daughters had left home?

It seemed unlikely. She had never made a move to keep any of them at home. Indeed, she had stayed a great deal in the background for most of their lives, as Leigh remembered it. Their father had dominated their lives more than anyone else. He had played with them and taken them everywhere.

She remembered Hawthorne holding a watercolor that she had brought home from school. 'Beautiful,' the big man had said, with

114

joy in his eyes. He had beamed at his sixth-grade daughter. 'Such talent you have.' Even at that age, Leigh's forms and choice of colors revealed an eye for appealing shapes and a taste that would develop.

Yes, Hawthorne had encouraged her. He had encouraged all his daughters, not just Hania. She remembered the way he had always cheered Claudia's athletic ability and how proud he was when they discovered she was an artist as well. Then, as robustly as Hawthorne Castle had lived, he died. A heart attack had taken him at age sixty-two.

And Sybil? Leigh strained to remember. She tried to think of anything that might hint that Sybil had not cared about them and would leave Hania the inheritance. But it just wouldn't come.

Leigh clenched a fist as the magazine slipped to the floor. She wrinkled her brow, trying to remember something. She'd never thought about it much before, but she did recall it had struck her as odd that Sybil had not gone back to Denver, where she was from, not even once to Leigh's knowledge. But then, why should she? Her girlhood friends had probably grown up and moved away.

Leigh was distracted from her thoughts by the door's opening and Braden's reappearing.

He wore a bandage on his left temple which made him look rakish, and Leigh could not suppress a grin.

'How is the wound?' she asked, getting up from the couch and tossing the unread magazine aside.

'He'll be fine,' said Dr. Thomas, emerging from behind Braden and taking the hand Leigh offered. 'A bump on the head, that's all.'

She smiled at the sturdy old man, who was half a head shorter than Braden. 'Thank you for taking care of him, Dr. Thomas,' Leigh said.

'Oh, I didn't do anything,' the older man said. 'He was well cared for already by the time he got to me.'

Braden winked at her. 'I had a very good nurse.'

'Oh, you mean the burly forest ranger who doctored him up,' she teased.

Braden thanked Dr. Thomas, then joked, 'I hope I don't have to see you again soon.'

'At least not professionally,' said Dr. Thomas. 'And don't go running down any more mountains.'

They laughed and walked out the front door and down the steps to the sidewalk. The Wagoneer was parked a few feet away, between a blue VW and a Chevy station wagon.

They drove to the house and stopped at the entrance. When Braden started to get out of the car, she put a hand on his arm, restraining him. 'I'll just hop out. Don't want the patient to exert himself.'

He scowled at her, and Leigh guessed he wasn't particularly in the mood for teasing. Before she got out, he put his hand on her arm. While she realized that the family must know by now whom she was spending her time with, she did not want to make a scene in front of the house. As she started to withdraw, he caught her chin with his hand, holding her a moment longer.

'I'll call you later,' he said, his long, dark eyelashes veiling his eyes slightly as he gazed into her brown eyes.

She left Braden and went up the steps, noticing on her way that it hadn't seemed to have rained there as much. A squirrel darted in front of her and ran around the side of the house.

Entering the house, she found it relatively quiet. She headed toward the kitchen, suddenly realizing how hungry she was. Hearing voices from the dining room, she glanced in and saw that Hania and Claudia were setting the table. For a moment, she was reminded of another time.

They were all younger, and Sybil was

setting the table. Leigh followed her around the table, taking pieces of silverware from the felt-lined box and reaching up to put the knives, forks, and spoons in their places.

'Not that side of the plate, Leigh, this side.' Her mother guided her hand so that Leigh placed the spoon next to the knife on a linen napkin.

'Uh, huh,' Leigh nodded, looking up at her mother. How beautiful, she thought, the sparkling silver and the delicate white china, with figures painted on the rims, and her mother so at ease, placing each object on the table where it belonged.

Leigh gave a start. Her sisters couldn't see her, for only part of the dining room was visible from where she stood, and they had moved around the table at the far end of the room.

She frowned. There was something else about that scene she needed to remember, though the memory wasn't as sharp as it had been a moment ago.

She had been small, of course, and she had been looking up at her mother. She had been happy, and she thought how much fun her mother must have had every time she set the table. Indeed, Sybil had smiled down at Leigh as she guided the smaller hand in placing the fork.

'How many places, Mother?' asked Leigh.

'One for each of us,' her mother said. But she had smiled and sighed as she went on. 'Your father, me, and you four girls.' Leigh thought she remembered her mother saying something else, but she couldn't remember what it was.

'Hi, sis,' called Claudia as she walked around the foot of the table and laid a plate where Braden had sat last night. The same plates, Leigh realized. It was the Lenox china that her mother had gotten on her seventeenth wedding anniversary, the year that Anastasia had been born. She remembered because Sybil always used to say that her daughter Anastasia was as old as the china. It was an heirloom now. It was also the china that Anastasia had wanted to use the night of the funeral.

'Where've you been?' asked Claudia, noticing the mud on the hem of Leigh's jeans.

'Oh, Braden and I went to the Cliff Dwellings, but we got caught in a storm. I must look a mess.' She pulled her hair back self-consciously.

She went upstairs to change, into beige rough-linen slacks and a maroon and beige overblouse. The sleeves hung wide at the wrist, giving her a somewhat Spanish look.

119

Except for the face, she thought, looking in the mirror at her freckles, bony nose and fly-away medium-brown hair. Dirty-dishwater brown, she used to call it.

She stepped into beige sandals and closed the door as she left her room. She walked down to the kitchen to help Hania and Claudia.

'What can I do?' she asked as she entered the kitchen and took a bowl of Jell-O out of the refrigerator.

'You can mix that up with whipped cream and this fruit. Then put it in the fridge again. It'll be dessert. It's Mrs. Garcia's night off.'

Leigh took the Jell-O to the kitchen table, where Claudia had already assembled heavy cream, a large bowl, and a beater. She enjoyed working with her sisters. Putting the beater into the cream, she realized that she felt closer to them than ever before. And now that they were adults, they didn't have to fight like children. Or, perhaps because their parents were both gone, they were unconsciously pulling together. All except Anastasia.

Where was she, anyway? Why was she so stand-offish? She rarely lowered herself to help with chores like preparing dinner, relying on Mrs. Garcia and Carlos to do all the work. Leigh realized she was being uncharitable, but it was the truth.

She looked at Hania, basting the chicken. Hania had always taken care of them when Sybil was busy. It seemed to Leigh that Anastasia had always helped as little as possible.

'If you don't move the beater back over the bowl, you're going to have whipped cream all over the table,' Claudia said.

Leigh came back to the present with a start. She must have been testing the thickness of the cream, for she was holding the beater in midair, and a large glob had gathered on the bottom of the beater. She lowered it into the bowl.

'It's almost ready,' said Hania, checking the chicken one last time. 'Is everyone here?'

Leigh thought Hania's voice shook a little, which was unusual for Hania. She had just been remembering how calm and responsible Hania had always been. She was probably just nervous and worried about what her sisters thought of her. Leigh knew that she would be less reticent if it weren't for Nathan. Poor Hania.

'I didn't see Anastasia,' said Leigh, realizing Hania had asked a question.

'Me either, but Richard's in the library reading the will again,' said Claudia. Then her face turned crimson as she realized that Hania might be embarrassed by any reference to it.

'We'll wait for half an hour,' said Hania. 'Leigh, would you . . . ' She hesitated, her cheeks turning unnaturally pink.

'I'll go ask Richard where Anastasia is,' volunteered Leigh, realizing that Hania did not want to confront Richard, who was obviously still angry with her over their dispute.

She wondered, as she left the kitchen and headed for the library, if Hania might decide to divide up the estate in spite of Nathan. After all, the inheritance was left to her, not to her husband.

Richard had not seen Anastasia, and twenty minutes later she had still not shown up. Leigh stood with Richard, Claudia, and Nathan in the dining room, sipping sherry. Claudia was talking quietly with Richard, whose back was turned to Nathan. Nathan was saying that they should go ahead with dinner.

'Dinner's always at seven,' he complained, his face looking pinched.

Hania came through the door from the kitchen, an anxious look on her face. Her eyes flitted over the company, and when she spoke, she seemed to be addressing no one in particular.

'Let's start,' she said. 'That is,' she murmured, 'if you don't mind, Richard.' She looked at the floor, and Leigh noticed the napkin she wrung in her hands. Leigh studied her face, realizing that Hania was upset over more than a delayed dinner.

'Yes, let's,' agreed Leigh, trying to ease the tension in the room. 'Anastasia can grab a snack later.'

Claudia bit her lip, holding her glass in one hand, with her arms crossed in front of one another. She flicked her eyes at Richard, who rocked on his heels. He looked a little pale against his white shirt collar and light-blue suit. Perhaps he was worried about his wife's whereabouts. But if so, he wasn't saying anything.

Nathan held out a chair for Leigh. 'Let's sit down,' he said. 'Dinner will be cold.' His cheeks had a tinge of pink. No, Leigh thought, things had not yet returned to normal.

Richard cleared his throat and pulled out his chair. Leigh looked at the end of the table where Braden had sat the night he dined with them. She pressed her lips together, thinking she had become too used to his presence. Soon she would have to go back to New York. What of Braden then? Had her feelings for him been born of frustration and need at a time of crisis? It frightened her to think so. Still, she knew she had given herself to

Braden because he made her feel safe that night. She had trusted him.

But there were still the doubts about his involvement in her mother's will. She tried to quell them as she passed a bowl of mashed potatoes to Nathan.

They ate mostly in silence. As she slowly chewed her chicken, Leigh found her thoughts returning to her parents. Funny, now that she was a woman herself, she wondered how such an exuberant, loving man could have been happy with such a reserved, undemonstrative woman. For the Sybil Castle Leigh knew had never been overt with her affections. She wondered if she'd been that way when Hawthorne met her. Something underlying Sybil's actions as wife and mother made Leigh feel she had never really known her.

For the first time, Leigh wondered why Sybil and Hawthorne had married. She realized she knew little about their courtship and marriage — only that Sybil had been the daughter of a railroad man. She hadn't had much money when she was younger but had studied to be a schoolteacher.

Leigh did know that Hawthorne had come to Culver City with cousin Charlie to make his fortune in the copper-mining business. Leigh glanced at the well-appointed dining room. He'd made that fortune. And Charlie had done equally well.

Cobwebs, thought Leigh, shaking her head. Did every meal around this table have to send her off on a tangent? And for what purpose? To try and understand Sybil's actions regarding her will? Yes, that was partly it. Now that the shock was over, Leigh found herself asking the same question everyone else was. For the will seemed so cruel and confusing.

Oh, Mother, she moaned inwardly. Why did you do it?

[Journal Entry]   **February 28, 1939**

I refused to eat downstairs tonight. Hawthorn and Charlie Sutter were there. Later, I listened to them at the door of the library. They told Father about their plan for a copper-mining business and they asked him if he would lend them the money to buy it. Hawthorne asked where I was. Charlie was very loud and drunk and asked where Anna and Sylvie, our maids, were. Then they said some vulgar things, so I went back upstairs.

— S.P.

7

'It's just that Anastasia's missing.' Leigh spoke in a low voice on the phone in the library. Braden had called after dinner. At first his tone had been warm and light; now it took on a clipped, anxious quality.

'Since when?' he asked.

'Well, she didn't show up for dinner. Richard didn't know where she was.'

'She couldn't have gone somewhere to visit someone?'

'I don't think so. She doesn't have any friends here.'

He paused, considering. 'May I come over?'

'Of course.'

'All right. I'll be there in a little while. And don't worry. Maybe she'll have turned up by the time I get there.'

Leigh put the white telephone back in its cradle and leaned on the edge of the large walnut desk. She remembered what he had said as they stood on the hill that day after the funeral. He had told her that he'd seen disputes over inheritances like this before, and that they had all led to unpleasantness.

A chilling sensation ran down the back of Leigh's neck. Surely, Anastasia had just forgotten to tell anyone where she was going. Might she have run into someone she knew and visited too long, forgetting the time? Leigh frowned, twisting the phone cord around her fingers. That didn't really sound right. Anastasia had hated Culver City and considered herself better than anyone in it. Consequently she had no friends that Leigh knew of.

Leigh clasped her arms, mechanically rubbing the rough linen material of her sleeves. She was glad Braden was coming over. She still had mixed feelings about his interest in her family's affairs but it would be good to see him, to talk to him. She also wanted to make sure he was feeling all right after today's accident.

She went back to join the others in the living room, now feeling that something was very much amiss. Anastasia really had no reason to be anywhere in Culver City but here, unless she was up to something the rest of them knew nothing about.

Claudia looked comfortable in one of the wing chairs. She was reading a book, or at least looking at the pages. Hania sat on the sofa facing the windows across the room, her needlework in her lap, but she glanced up when Leigh came into the room. Richard paced back and forth near the mantel, his pipe clenched between his teeth. Nathan stood by the small writing desk, fingering the change in his pocket. Not a very cheerful group.

What did Nathan have to be mournful about? Leigh wondered in a moment of irritation. Then she stopped herself, realizing she was following a train of thought that had to do with the inheritance, and that wasn't the problem at hand.

The clock ticking on the mantel marked every second. It would probably take Braden ten minutes to drive here. Leigh decided to make a cup of tea just to pass the time.

Turning back into the hall, she went to the kitchen. It seemed more peaceful there, away from the living room, where the atmosphere was so heavy, and she turned on the fire under a tea kettle. She sat at the table and stared idly at the old-fashioned paddle fan hanging from the ceiling. It moved slowly, as if caught by a draft.

A few minutes later, when she was sipping her tea, the doorbell rang. Braden. Claudia greeted him. Leigh carried her cup into the living room and felt a tiny thrill as her gaze locked with his. He had shaved and changed into a light-blue shirt, navy corduroy sport coat, and gray trousers.

Decisively he confronted the others. Richard came forward, and Braden spoke.

'When did you last see your wife?'

'Look here,' said Richard, 'who said you could walk in here and take over? It's none of your business where Anastasia is. None of yours.' He glanced emphatically at the family and walked back into the dining room, where he fixed himself a drink.

But Braden was not to be intimidated. 'You're right,' he said. 'But you yourself must be concerned. There aren't that many places in this town where she could be, are there?'

Leigh watched Richard put ice in a glass. Whiskey followed, and he tossed down the drink before answering. His hand shook. Then she saw the red that climbed up from the collar of his shirt to his hair. She had never thought of it before, but could it be possible that Anastasia had a lover, and her absence was embarrassing to Richard?

In Culver City? Ridiculous. If Anastasia were to take a lover, he would most likely be in a far more exotic place than her home town.

Richard turned to Braden, a slight twitch in his left cheek revealing his nervousness. 'I can't imagine where she might have gone,' he said. He seemed to be fighting himself in

130

admitting he was worried.

Leigh watched as Braden's determination and certainty overcame Richard's evasiveness and mistrust.

Richard finally gave up. 'What do you suggest?' he asked.

Braden's shoulders relaxed a fraction of an inch, as if he thought half the battle had been won. He turned to the others, and his glance rested a moment on each family member. Nathan rubbed the fingers of his left hand together, as if kneading a piece of thread. Hania still mechanically worked her needle-point, but Leigh noticed her hands were shaking. Claudia had shut the book with a marker in it and frowned.

Leigh realized that Braden was staring at her. She stiffened under his glance. He was scrutinizing her carefully as well. Then quickly the look passed, and he questioned Richard again.

'When did you last see your wife?'

'At breakfast, I believe. She said she had some errands to do.'

'I see,' said Braden. 'And you did not accompany her?'

'No. I went to Nathan's club and played nine holes of golf, ate lunch, then came back here.'

Braden turned to the others. 'Anybody else

131

see her after that?'

Claudia scratched her head. 'I wasn't here for lunch either. Went to see old friends and ate at the . . . Wait a minute. I passed her car on the Lordsburg Highway as I was coming home. At least I think I did. It was the rented Lincoln.'

'We saw the Lincoln too,' Leigh reminded Braden. 'Or a car like it in the parking lot at the Cliff Dwellings when we went up.'

Braden acknowledged her, then turned to Richard. 'If she went out today in your car, how did you get to the club?'

'Nathan lent me the Datsun.'

'How about you, Hania?' Braden asked gently.

She shook her head, only raising her eyes long enough to answer Braden's question. 'Nathan and I ate lunch here. We were alone.'

That would make sense, because Hania usually drove the Datsun, Leigh thought.

'I see,' said Braden. Then after a moment, he said, 'I think we should go look for her.'

Richard, now regaining control, said, 'That's what I was thinking. We must organize a search and decide where she might have gone. Perhaps she drove off somewhere and had car trouble.'

'Wouldn't she call?' asked Leigh.

'Not if she's been hurt,' said Braden.

132

Leigh flashed him a look that said, Why upset Richard if it's not necessary? After all, they didn't yet know if anything had happened to Anastasia or if she was merely playing truant. But then, she thought she understood Braden's tactics. He wanted to shock Richard into reacting. Perhaps Braden thought Richard was hiding something and it needed to be jarred loose.

She watched Richard's face, usually so set in its expressions. His eyes darted from Braden to the floor, and around the living room. His right eyelid still twitched. But he made an attempt at bravado.

'Of course,' he said, clearing his throat. 'We'll search at once. If she's in danger or can't reach a phone . . . ' He let the sentence trail off as everyone rose.

'Richard can come with me,' said Claudia. 'I'll just get my keys.' She left the room in search of her handbag.

Leigh and Braden looked at each other, knowing they would go together. But where would they go?

'Nathan, you or Hania call the highway patrol and the hospital,' said Braden, 'just in case there's been an accident. Then drive downtown and inquire at the police station. Ask any of the proprietors who are still open if they've seen her or the car.'

'Well, I don't think — ' Nathan protested, not wanting the family name besmirched. But Braden's look stopped him.

'Surely there's no reason to get the police involved,' Richard interjected.

'If she's really missing, we'll need to let them know,' said Braden, overriding any argument. Richard acquiesced, and Claudia, returning with her car keys, motioned for him to follow her out. She glanced at Braden for instructions.

'Search the outside of the house first,' he said to Claudia. 'Then the rest of the neighborhood. She might have had trouble nearby.'

Claudia and Richard looked at each other. Leigh's pulse quickened. Culver City was such a peaceful, isolated town. One just didn't think of mishaps occurring here. She went to get a wool jacket and put on more practical shoes. It would be cold if they were going to be out long.

After the others had left, Braden glanced around the living room, then when Leigh returned, they went to the car. The stars were bright above, and their footsteps crunched on the gravel drive.

'Where are we going?' asked Leigh as they got in, noticing he had brought the Wagoneer rather than the Volvo. He must have anticipated trouble when she'd spoken to him on the phone.

He gave her a sidelong glance as he started the car. 'I think we should drive farther out of town. I'd like to go by the cemetery, for one thing.'

'The cemetery. Why?'

'Was Anastasia upset over your mother's death?' he asked in lieu of giving her an answer.

Leigh had to think for a moment. She had been so ashamed of her own lack of grief that she hadn't paid much attention to anyone else's response before the will was read.

'Well, I guess not. Of course you saw how she reacted to the will.'

'Yes. That's what bothers me.'

'How do you mean?'

'She and Richard wanted to contest the will. But you didn't, nor did Claudia. Your reactions were entirely different.'

Leigh chewed on her lip, then said, 'You told us there was nothing we could do, and besides, my own thoughts and emotions weren't sorted out. I guess I just made up my mind that it was my mother's business.' Or had she simply put up a barrier because it was too painful to contemplate the fact that Sybil might not have loved her younger daughters or had actually resented them for some reason and therefore cut them out of the will?

'But why the cemetery?' she asked, returning to the issue at hand.

'A wild hunch maybe, but you said Anastasia and Sybil were close. You also said your sister was rather unpredictable. Might she go to the grave site alone in some kind of attempt to communicate with your mother's spirit? Perhaps seeking some enlightenment about the will?'

Leigh's skin crawled. 'Anastasia does do eccentric things sometimes, and she's adamant about the will, but she's not crazy. I doubt she'd go to Mother's grave at night.' Her sister might be a prima donna, but Leigh did not think she was mad.

They drove through the quiet town and out the highway toward the cemetery. The moon was low on the horizon, giving the mountains in the distance an inky color. By the side of the road twisted cholla plants gripped the hillside as if tortured by unknown elements.

Leigh realized her body was clenched. She certainly never would come out to the cemetery alone at night. She was not sure whether she was glad to be with Braden or not.

He pulled off the narrow highway onto the muddy road that led to the Catholic cemetery. A gate barred their way.

'Come on,' he said as he switched off the motor. 'We'll have to walk.'

Leigh shivered. But she opened her door and stepped down. Immediately her shoes sank into the mud. She jumped when Braden gripped her arm. 'Stay close to me,' he said.

He climbed over the bar that prevented cars from entering the cemetery, then helped Leigh over. Beyond the archway, the road swung to the right and then left. White crosses leaned close to the road, reaching out to passers-by. Now she could see the tombstones and colorful shapes of Madonnas and wreaths, made weird by the dark shadows of the night. Her teeth chattered as she pointed toward Sybil's grave.

'Ov — over there, isn't it?' she said.

He nodded and pulled her to him. Ordinarily, Leigh would have found comfort in the curve of his arm, but in the eerie setting, his grip on her shoulder made her shake even more.

They left the road and walked between the gravestones toward the Castle plot. 'Careful,' said Braden, stopping suddenly and jostling her to one side.

Leigh opened her mouth to scream but clapped her hands over her mouth instead. An open grave faced them, freshly dug for a funeral that was probably tomorrow.

'Oh, no,' she whispered as a feeling of hysteria gripped her.

Braden relaxed his hold on her and turned his head to look around. They passed along a path lined with a low hedge and came to Sybil's grave, but besides the flowers and wreaths left by mourners, there was nothing. The moon was nearly full, and Leigh's eyes had adjusted to the night. She could see everything clearly — the tombstones, as if they had been thrown at random in a field; the mounds of dirt over new graves; wilted flowers in vases; forgotten wreaths with fronds moving in the breeze.

'Let's go,' Braden said, almost sounding disappointed. 'She's not here.'

Leigh was only too glad to leave. They carefully stepped over brush that had fallen onto the path and found their way back to the road. Leigh followed Braden, and while she was glad he led the way, she felt as if someone might be watching from behind. It made her want to turn around and see, but at the same time, she was too frightened.

They hurried along the muddy road, crawled over the bar, then Braden stood for a moment gazing back at the cemetery. Leigh leaned against the Wagoneer's hood, watching

138

him. He shook his head, as if puzzling over something.

Finally he returned to the car, and gratefully, Leigh got in. He turned the car around, and as they approached the road, their headlights illuminated the orderly Masonic tombstones across the road. Like soldiers they stood, guarding their graves, solid, complete, not needing any ornament other than the overhanging trees.

Leigh let out a long breath. She looked at Braden and swallowed. 'Your theory was wrong.' She heard the tightness in her voice and knew she hadn't meant to sound reproachful. It was just that she had had difficulty understanding why Anastasia would be at the cemetery in the first place, or why Braden had thought to look for her there.

They were at the edge of the highway. If they turned left, they would return to town. But the highway to the right led on out past the old silver mine. As if reading her thoughts, Braden said, 'The old silver mine's out this way, isn't it?'

'Yes,' she said, 'but why go out there?'

He had already swung the wagon onto the highway. 'Because Claudia saw her driving in this direction.'

'Her car anyway,' said Leigh, not sure why

she said it that way. 'What about the Cliff Dwellings?'

'Yes. It might have been Anastasia on the path in the rain, though she didn't stop when I called out. We'll look there after we check the mine. Though I hate the thought of searching the Cliff Dwellings at night. That trail won't be safe in the dark.'

They drove about a mile, then slowed. 'It's here, isn't it?'

Leigh squinted into the darkness, trying to recognize the turnoff. Then she saw it. A weather-beaten sign with chipped paint pointed out the road to the Santa Maria Silver Mine. It was abandoned now. The buildings that used to house the miners, the old saloon and the office were all bleached and rotted by the elements — shells now, clinging perilously to the mountainside.

Gravel crunched under the tires as they drove slowly up the curving road, and rocks flew up to hit the undercarriage. The road was not often traveled, but curious tourists did visit the place from time to time.

Braden pulled up in front of the office. 'There might be someone about,' he said.

'Old Man Martin,' said Leigh. 'He and his wife used to live out here and answer questions asked by the tourists, but that was ten years ago. I don't know if they're still here.' She was a little less frightened of being at the mine than at the cemetery, though this was another place she would never visit alone at night.

He turned off the motor, then reached across her to the glove compartment. Flipping it open, he rummaged around for a flashlight. After testing it, he got out of the car, and Leigh followed.

They tried the office, but it was locked, and no one answered their calls. Braden flicked his light over the buildings and up the road where it led around the mountain. They would have to be careful where they walked.

Funny, she and Anastasia had often come here together as teen-agers. The thought chilled her now.

Braden took her hand, but its warmth was no longer reassuring. She still could not understand his intuition, or whatever it was that had led him here. She held onto his hand tightly though, to help keep her balance on the rocky road.

They followed the road around the side of the hill, passing two buildings on the left. Ahead a tall wooden structure teetered next to an abandoned excavation. It was curious to think that this place was once alive and producing millions.

Her foot slipped, and she clutched Braden

for support. He stopped to let her get her footing. But she heard him emit a wordless sound, and she squinted her eyes toward the beam that spilled off the side of the road down the edge of the excavation. She couldn't see what he was looking at.

'Stay here,' he commanded, and she felt him tense his muscles as he pulled away from her.

'No,' she said, shivering. 'What is it?'

He had already let go of her hand, however, and stepped forward, his boots crunching on the rocks. Leigh followed.

Then she saw. Extending upward was a hand reaching out near the edge of the excavation, the fingers clutching the air.

'Oh, no,' whispered Leigh, her legs becoming rubber. She tried to approach, but shock and fear held her back. For she could see the rest now.

Wool skirt up over one knee, the other leg flung across a piece of old lumber, face smudged with dirt, eyes staring lifelessly into the flashlight, Anastasia's body clung to the sloping ground.

8

'She's dead,' said Braden after getting up from where he had knelt to inspect the body. Leigh crept closer, shock still gripping her. She was afraid to move too close, for the loose dirt of the excavation was dangerous, and from the edge of the road they could not see the bottom. But they could see Anastasia in the beam of the flashlight. A deep gash had laid her forehead open, and her head was pressed on its side into the dirt. She was sprawled as if she had frozen in that position while crawling up to the road. Leigh felt sick and bent double, clutching her stomach. She had never seen a victim of violent death before. And this was her own sister.

Braden came to her and steadied her while she gagged at the side of the road.

'I'm all right,' she said when she could speak, standing up and leaning against him. Waves of hot and cold passed over her, and she thought she would be sick again. Braden held her to him and guided her back up the road. With an effort, she commanded her feet to take her.

It seemed like hours before they got to the

car, and then she must have fainted, because when she opened her eyes, her head was on the back of the seat, and they were parked in the driveway in front of the house. Braden was chafing her hand with his.

'Are you all right?' he asked as she opened her eyes.

She parted her dry lips and mumbled.

'I've got to find Richard, tell him,' he said.

'Ummm,' Leigh mumbled, grasping for the door handle. 'I'll come. Poor Richard.' How awful. What would he do?

Braden hurried around to Leigh's side of the car as she got out, and she leaned on him as they walked to the porch. He pushed open the door, and they were in the hallway, the bright lights from the living room blinding them.

Richard got up from a chair and came toward them. Braden's voice was hoarse as he said, 'I'm sorry, Richard. It's bad . . . we found her, and she's . . . she's dead . . . I wish I could tell you otherwise.'

Richard looked at Braden for a few seconds in disbelief, then he turned away and gripped the back of a chair with his hands, lowering his head as his shoulders convulsed.

'I told her, I told her,' he moaned quietly, shaking his head.

'Told her what?' asked Braden, taking a step closer.

Richard pushed himself away from the chair. 'Nothing,' he said, his face a white mask of pain. 'Take me to her. Where is she?' He looked at Braden then, and Leigh saw the helplessness in his eyes. It was the first time she had seen him lose his composure completely.

'I'm sorry, Richard,' she said, putting a hand on his arm. She tried to comfort him, but she herself was in such deep shock she could do little. Movements were blurred, and she was dimly aware of Braden's voice in the background, of the other family members passing in and out of her vision. Braden told her she should stay at the house, but she shook her head. They got into the car and drove back to the mine.

*   *   *

Dawn was just lifting the night's dark cover by the time Leigh returned to the house. Braden went on to the sheriff's office for questioning, since he had found the body. Leigh was too tired to think anymore. But she couldn't stop replaying the horrible scene over and over in her mind. They had called the sheriff at his home, and within half an hour he and his men had met them at the scene of the accident.

Leigh had waited with Claudia in the car until she began to feel stifled and needed some air.

'I can't breathe,' she had told her sister, and Claudia had gotten out with her to walk part way up the rocky road to where the sheriff's men were pulling Anastasia's body from the excavation.

Braden's boots had crunched on gravel as he came to where Leigh and Claudia were standing. Claudia, dazed, dropped Leigh's hand, which she was clutching, and moved aside to allow him to speak privately to Leigh.

'What was she doing out here dressed in street clothes?' Leigh had asked. 'It must have been hard to walk on this road in those heels. Braden, I think something's terribly wrong.' She put one hand to her forehead, closing her eyes as if the scene would be more understandable when she reopened them.

Braden had mumbled something unintelligible, but Leigh heard him say, 'Like I thought.' Then he spoke to Claudia, who was staring at the body as if in disbelief. From her baffled expression, it was apparent that she was as perplexed as Leigh.

Floodlights had covered the area, illuminating the spooky gloom. The shock of the accident was still with them as they stood together viewing the scene.

They had remained there several hours while the sheriff's men went over the ground. Now Claudia and Leigh stumbled into the house, each heading in a different direction for warmth and comfort — Claudia to soak in a hot bath and Leigh to make a fresh pot of steaming tea, although she seriously doubted that any liquid could warm the coldness that pervaded her soul.

In the living room, Leigh found Hania and Nathan sitting together on the sofa, holding hands. Hania's face was haggard and wet with tears. Hania and Nathan had come home from the search after the others and had not gone to the scene of the accident when the sheriff phoned. Leigh went to Hania and sat on her other side, trying to find words to comfort her older sister. She didn't know how Hania felt about Anastasia. It was, nonetheless, a tragedy, and Leigh was sure that Hania shared the horror she felt.

Leigh mumbled her words of regret, then left the couple to their solitude. She climbed the stairs with her teacup and took it to her bedroom.

Opening the door, she set the cup down on her dresser, then pulled off her jacket, sweater, and pants. She sat for a long time sipping tea on the edge of her bed, her mind a blank, her hands still clammy. Then pulling back the covers on the narrow bed, she crawled between cool sheets. Images spun in her mind before sleep took her.

When she opened her eyes, light was spilling through the curtains. She shook her head. From the shadows it cast, she could tell it was afternoon light. Reaching for her clock, she found she was right. It was one o'clock. She had slept six hours in spite of the gruesome events of the past night. Her body felt somewhat rested, but her mind was still groggy. Perhaps she didn't want to wake up, didn't want to face the horrible truth. For the second time in a week, shock stifled her feelings, and her mind moved of its own accord, observing, piecing facts together.

When she first saw Anastasia, Leigh had wondered what killed her. Could she just have fallen? The hilly terrain and the disguised edge of the mountain road could easily have caused such an accident.

It struck Leigh now that Anastasia had been lying in an odd position, almost as if she had been trying to climb out of the excavation but had lost consciousness from a blow to her head. Or perhaps she had lost her footing on the rubble and simply fallen, knocked herself out, and slid. Either way, the question remained — why was she at the mine in the first place? She certainly couldn't have been hiking, clothed as she was in a dress and street shoes.

Leigh rubbed her head and got out of bed as the questions bubbled up in her mind.

She heard voices as she descended the stairs. When she reached the bottom, she could see that Sheriff McElroy stood by the mantel, talking in a low voice to Claudia, who sat on the sofa. Sybil's portrait above them made a macabre counterpoint. Leigh glared at the painting, angry at her mother at that moment, wishing the painting were alive, wanting to grasp the smooth folds of the silk dress and shake her.

She glanced down at Claudia, whose profile reflected Sybil's three-quarter pose. But Claudia was not smugly silent like the picture. Her conversation reserved nothing, hid nothing.

'I'm sorry,' said Leigh from the arched entrance to the living room. 'I didn't mean to interrupt.'

'Come on in, Miss Leigh,' said the sheriff, shifting his bulk and scratching his thining hair. 'Your sister and I weren't discussing anything private. I'm just awful sorry about Miss Anastasia.' He cleared his throat, looking ill at ease.

'Thank you, Sheriff,' Leigh acknowledged. She rubbed her hands. 'the house feels so cold. I was just going to make some coffee. Would either of you like some?'

Claudia spoke. 'No thanks, sis. We had some earlier.'

Leigh had started for the kitchen but paused and looked at the sheriff. He had held his job since before she could remember, and no one seemed to have found fault with his abilities. Of course there hadn't been many violent deaths in the county. Mostly just drunken driving or an occasional theft, as far as she knew. She wondered how he felt about his present case.

'Sheriff,' she said, leaning on the edge of a wing chair, 'do you think it was an accident? I mean, could someone have pushed her off that road?' She felt the goose bumps rise on her flesh as she said it.

'I don't think anything yet, ma'am. But we're checking all the possibilities. Perhaps you have some information that might be helpful. Do you know why Miss Anastasia might have been at the old mine? Seems an odd thing to have gone there dressed like that.'

Leigh nodded. 'We've all been thinking the same thing. No, I don't know why she would have gone there. Has the time of death been established?'

'She was, er, that is, she died between two and four o'clock in the afternoon according to Doc. Did you see her earlier yesterday?'

The same question Braden had asked. 'No, I didn't. Oh, wait, yes, I did. Braden and I left here yesterday morning for a hike. I saw Anastasia watching us from the window.' She shivered as she remembered Anastasia's malevolent look.

'Hmmm,' said the sheriff. 'And she didn't ever say what her plans were for the day?'

'No.' Leigh felt ashamed that she hadn't taken more interest in her sister's activities. If she had, she might have been able to prevent this from happening.

'She did seem upset about the will,' Leigh finally said.

'Yes,' Sheriff McElroy said, looking toward the windows. 'So I've heard. That is, Mr. Lancaster told me that.'

'Does he ... ' Leigh stopped. 'Do you think my sister's accident had something to do with the will?'

'Too early to say. First things first. I'll need you girls to stay in town for a few days. I'd like to get the matter cleared up before you leave. There may be an inquest.'

Leigh's heart thudded. An inquest. They would be the center of attention. She glanced quickly at Claudia, whose eyes were large.

151

'I'll contact my office in Albuquerque and tell them I'll be staying,' said Claudia, getting up and straightening her skirt.

'Thank you,' said McElroy. 'I may have to bother you folks again if I have any more questions.' He headed toward the hallway, then stopped. 'By the way,' he said to Leigh as she got out of her chair. 'You were with Lancaster, weren't you?'

She nodded.

'Would you mind telling me where you'd been just before you found the, er, body?'

Leigh's heart pumped blood at an increasing rate. 'We had gone to look for Anastasia. Braden picked me up here and we drove out to the, um, cemetery.' She shot Claudia a look and saw her sister stop in the doorway to the dining room and look back questioningly.

'The cemetery?' asked McElroy sharply. 'What for?'

'Well, Braden didn't really know where to look. He had some notion that Anastasia might be trying to communicate with Mother's spirit, to try to make sense out of the will, I suppose.'

'Was your sister the type who believed in ghosts?' he asked.

'I don't know,' she said and glanced at Claudia. 'We weren't that close. It's been five years since we were last together.'

152

Sheriff McElroy moved a step closer and lowered his voice. 'Has any of the family mentioned any sort of odd occurrence since Sybil died? God rest her soul.'

'You mean, has any of us seen a ghost?' Leigh queried.

'Something like that,' said the sheriff.

Claudia watched curiously as she waited for her sister to answer.

Leigh thought of the presence she had felt the night she'd come home. It was possible that Sybil's spirit did indeed haunt them in some way. But she was unwilling to communicate this to the sheriff.

'No,' she said.

McElroy relaxed his shoulders. 'Well, I'd like to know why Lancaster took you out there last night. I think I'll have another word with him.' He lowered his voice still further. 'If I were you, ma'am, I'd be careful. You too, miss,' he said, nodding his head in Claudia's direction.

'We will,' said Leigh, escorting him to the door. She was more than ready for him to leave.

After he had gone, she returned to the living room, where Claudia was clearing away the coffee cups. Leigh followed her to the kitchen. Claudia's back was to her as she put the milk in the container and said softly, 'You

153

didn't tell me that about the cemetery. Strange, don't you think?'

'That Braden would want to look there? I suppose so.' She shrugged. 'I think I need a cup of coffee. I've got a headache.'

She turned the fire on under the coffeepot to warm it. Outside, the sky seemed to darken. It was unusual for them to have so few bright days. Late autumn in New Mexico was usually delightful.

Leigh knew Claudia was waiting for an explanation, but she wasn't sure she could give it. Why had Braden wanted to go to the cemetery? Was it really logical? And then driving Leigh out to the mine; he had been the one to discover Anastasia's body. How had he known they would find her there?

Leigh took a deep breath as she poured the coffee. Claudia had sat down at the kitchen table with her hands folded in front of her. Leigh took her cup to the table and pulled out a chair to sit opposite her.

For a moment they were silent, then Leigh spoke, slowly at first. 'I have no idea what to think.'

'No one does.'

'Braden was worried that something might happen, but I don't think he suspected anything like this.'

'Why, because of the will?'

Leigh nodded. 'Yes. He said something always happens when there's a dispute over an unusual inheritance. But I thought he was more concerned that someone might harm Hania. I don't see what Anastasia had to do with it.' She told Claudia about her conversation with Braden on the hill behind the house the day of the funeral.

'Awful, isn't it?' said Claudia, more to herself than to Leigh.

'Of course.'

'I mean greed or whatever causes people to do such things.'

'Yes, but that doesn't explain it. Hania got the estate. Yet she's been in no danger.'

'None that we know of,' said Claudia.

'No.' Leigh looked at Claudia curiously.

Then Claudia asked, 'So you don't think this accident was what Braden expected?'

Leigh felt a tingle at the back of her neck. 'I don't know. I shouldn't think he knew what to expect exactly. Still, it does seem strange . . . ' She drifted off.

'Hmmm,' said Claudia.

Leigh was not sure she wanted to articulate the rest of her thought. It was strange that Braden knew almost exactly where to look for Anastasia. She drummed her fingers beside her coffee cup.

'I know it looks suspicious, doesn't it? The

fact that we found her, and Braden was the first one there.'

'Oh, sis,' said Claudia. 'That could have happened to any of us. After all, we were all looking for her. It would have been the same regardless of who found her.'

'Maybe.' Leigh felt a knot in her chest. She knew Claudia's words were meant to be comforting. But there were too many unanswered questions. She changed the subject. 'Is Mrs. Garcia cooking tonight?'

Claudia shrugged. 'I don't know if anyone feels like eating. I'll tell her to put out some sandwiches at seven.'

'OK,' said Leigh. 'By the way, where is Hania?'

'I don't know. Upstairs with Nathan, I think. I didn't talk to her much after the — that is . . . '

'I know.' Leigh hadn't seen much of Hania either. 'Well, I think I'll freshen up and maybe have a walk before dinner,' she continued.

Leigh went upstairs, feeling like her limbs were made of lead. She forced herself into the shower. All the time, bits of thoughts and mental pictures floated through her mind with no logic but their own.

She thought of Braden, and how his nearness affected her, and she felt embarrassed that with so much tragedy around her, she could think of romance. Her skin tingled as she remembered his hands brushing her cheek as he'd said good night the night they had dinner. Then she brought her thoughts under control. This seemed a bad time to contemplate a relationship. Perhaps because she was unsure of Braden's part in all this?

Though she hated to admit it, she knew she was suspicious. She wanted to trust him, but there was too much as yet unclear about his relationship to the will. She didn't know him well enough to assess whether he was being completely frank with her or holding something back. She wanted to find that out before she allowed herself to grow any closer to him.

She toweled herself dry and put on a cotton wraparound dress with wide, loose sleeves. The subdued lavender color suited her mood, while the full skirt and sleeves allowed her freedom of movement. She combed her hair and applied lipstick and blusher, as much to cheer herself as to improve her appearance.

No sooner had she descended the stairs than she saw Claudia opening the front door to Braden. He exchanged a few words with Claudia, and Leigh couldn't help but notice how at ease with her he seemed to be. He kept his voice low, and Claudia leaned her head forward to answer him in a spontaneous easy manner.

That's it, thought Leigh with an uneasy feeling in her stomach. He makes people trust him. He seems so sincere, so caring, with that endearing smile.

She had no more time for contemplation, however, as Braden came over to her. Her heart skipped a beat. Surely she had been foolish to let her imagination run away with her. He was guilty of nothing except stealing her heart.

'I wanted to see if you were all right,' he said as Claudia left them.

'Yes.' She looked away, unable to meet his eyes. She was sure the doubts she felt would show, and she wasn't prepared to explain herself just yet.

But with the tips of his fingers, he brought her chin around to face him. Slowly she lifted her lids. Seeing her troubled expression, he lifted an eyebrow and reached for her waist.

Involuntarily she stiffened. But he grasped her with both hands and made her look at him. 'Leigh.' His voice was hushed, intimate.

'I — ' she began. But he cut her off by placing his fingers on her lips.

'Something's wrong,' he said. 'You're worried.'

'Yes, of course . . . '

He squared his shoulders and released her. 'About your sister.'

She nodded.

'Where can we talk? I've got my car if you . . . '

'No,' she cut him off. 'That is, I'm sure we can talk in the library.'

'All right.' He nodded gravely and let her lead him across the hallway. She pushed open the heavy oak doors, and they stepped across the mahogany borders of the parquet floor onto the Aubusson rug that covered the main area of the room.

She walked over to the heavy draperies to pull them open, revealing arched windows with leaded glass. Dusk left most of the room in shadow. Leigh sat in one of the large leather chairs, and Braden leaned on the big walnut desk in the center of the room. The fireplace at the end of the room was cold, and Leigh wondered idly why no one ever made a fire.

'I was afraid of this,' he said.

'Afraid of what?' She looked up.

He stared out the window at the drive in front of the house and at the garden in the center of the horseshoe drive, no longer in bloom. A gust of wind lifted several leaves and blew them away. 'You doubt me,' he said.

She felt angry at him, blushing at the same time. 'I'm sorry, but there have been two deaths in my family. This is hardly the time for an involvement.'

'I would think just the opposite.'

'What do you mean?'

He moved toward her then, reaching for her hands, but Leigh held back. 'We need to work together, Leigh. I want to protect you. I want to share your grief.'

'But how can you?' She felt tears of anger threaten to spill from her eyes; her only defense was to attack.

He turned his back, and she knew she'd hurt him. But she couldn't help it. She felt very vulnerable. She didn't want to think of Braden in a romantic way now. She was too nervous, and she didn't know why.

'I've got an idea,' he said, pivoting slowly to face her.

'What?'

'You'd like to know how your sister died, wouldn't you?'

'Of course.'

'Would you want to know even if it meant incriminating someone close to you?'

Horror struck at her heart. 'But it could have been an accident. No one's said she was . . . ' She hesitated. 'Murdered.'

He looked at her for a long moment, his

eyelids lowering to cover his gaze. Then he said in a voice that was low but firm. 'But if she was, could you stand to live with the possibility that one of your own family, or someone you are close to, is a murderer?'

She shook her head, her emotions choking her. 'No, no, of course not.'

He grasped her shoulders, then pulled her up, forcing her to look at him. 'Leigh, I want to get to the bottom of this as much as you do. I want you to trust me.'

Emotions pulled at her so that she grasped his shoulders with her hands. 'Where will it end? First, Mother's will, and now this.' To her own embarrassment, she started to cry, pouring out her grief and frustration at last. Braden held her to him, kissing her gently on her hair and face. Finally he dried her eyes with a handkerchief from his pocket, giving it to her to blow her nose in. Then, when she had spilled all her tears, he spoke.

'I'd like to help you and your family, Leigh. I care about you very much, darling. Will you let me do what I can to help get to the bottom of things?'

Leigh fought to stop her trembling. She wanted to place her faith in him. Until they came up with an explanation for these mysterious matters, her growing feelings for him would be thwarted by the shadows hanging over them. She could feel the conflict inside her. But finally she decided she must give in to Braden's request. If he had a way of uncovering the facts, she had to let him try, even if it meant incriminating someone close to her.

'Yes,' she whispered, her cheek against his shoulder. 'I want the truth.'

[Journal Entry]   **August 4, 1939**

Daddy is so ill it frightens me. The doctor says they've done all they can. But he looks so thin. I'm very scared. There's no one to help me.

Hawthorne Castle sat with me at the hospital, but I told him it was no use his being there for me, only if it was Father he cared about. He stayed anyway. Sometimes he takes my hand, but I can't feel anything. I like to be alone, but then I'm afraid what will happen.

— S.P.

9

Anastasia was buried next to Sybil in the family plot. Again the family assembled at the Catholic graveyard, in an eerie re-creation of the funeral that had brought Leigh home in the first place. This time, though, there were fewer mourners.

Afterward, Claudia and Leigh sat up talking late into the night. Claudia, who confessed that she too had shut a door on thoughts of her mother's will, was now confused and puzzled by Anastasia's death. She stared belligerently into the fire they had lighted to keep away the chill. She spread her hands in front of her, palms open. The fire snapped and crackled as it bit the dry juniper logs. She voiced what had been on Leigh's mind for some time now.

'If it wasn't an accident, and someone else killed her, why?' Claudia asked, her usually ruddy cheeks pale.

Leigh slowly shook her head, her elbows on her knees. She stared into the fire, as if an answer lay there. She thought over the occurrences since the family had been home. Richard and Anastasia had threatened to contest the will. Could Nathan have killed Anastasia in an attempt to foil her plans? Greed could be a powerful motive. It was possible.

Or was there some other explanation behind Anastasia's death? Could Richard have done it himself for some reason not apparent to the rest of them? After all, they really knew nothing about the couple's private life.

Braden had expected something to occur as a result of the family dispute. If there was going to be trouble, Braden had seemed to imply it would come from Anastasia and Richard's corner. But she was unlikely to cause any trouble now.

★   ★   ★

Leigh went into the library to see if she had left a book there the night before, when she hadn't been able to sleep. As she turned the brass knob on the door and pushed it inward, she stopped, surprised to see Richard bent over an open drawer at the right of the big walnut desk.

'Oh,' she said. 'I didn't know anyone was in here.'

Richard looked up and hastily shut the drawer. His dark brows furrowed slightly, and his face turned a light shade of crimson, as if she had caught him doing something he was trying to hide.

Her heart began to hammer, and she considered backing out of the room. But the damage was done, and she stood her ground. Better to act as casual as possible and reassure Richard that there was nothing unusual in his looking through the desk in a house that was not his own, she thought sardonically.

She cleared her throat as he came around the desk, drumming his fingers on the veneer. She closed the door behind her, letting her eyes roam around the room.

'I was looking for a book I thought I might have left here,' she said. 'Couldn't sleep last night.'

Richard shrugged and reached into his jacket pocket for his pipe and tobacco. She thought he might explain what he was doing, but he only frowned, fumbling with his tobacco pouch.

She decided to ask. 'Were you looking for something?'

He raised his aristocratic brows as if he had no idea what she was talking about, but Leigh was not about to fall for his pretense.

'When I came in, you seemed to be looking for something. Perhaps I can help you.'

'Oh.' He waved it away with his pipe hand. 'Stationery. I thought I might find something to jot a note on. I've run out.'

Leigh acknowledged that with a nod, but found it hard to believe he had been doing so much correspondence that he had run out of his own letterhead. She was sure he carried some in his briefcase.

'Well, I'm sure we can find some.' She walked to the desk. 'Let me see, you were looking here, weren't you?'

She fingered the brass knob on the top right-hand drawer, and it slid open easily. The drawer contained stationery in pale shades of pink and purple with matching envelopes. Leigh looked up innocently.

'Why, here's some.'

He shut his lips in a tight line, then opened them again, his dark eyes penetrating hers. 'Pink is hardly very masculine, wouldn't you agree?'

After a cursory glance at the other contents of the drawer, she shut it and shrugged. 'You're probably right.' Then she turned to the bookcase and picked out a likely title, pulling it from the shelf.

'Hmm, I must have put this back and then forgotten it.' She opened the book, then looked at Richard again. 'I suppose you'll be leaving soon.'

'Tomorrow,' he said, looking away from her. Leigh could see the shadows under his eyes and the red splotches on his face. Even though she would have liked to know why he was rummaging in Sybil's desk, she could hardly cross-examine him. Surely he must feel some grief over his wife's death. Her heart hammered at her next thought — what if he had killed her himself?

She studied the floral pattern in the thick Aubusson carpet, trying to steady herself. The idea that she might be standing in the same room with a murderer was not exactly comforting. She couldn't begin to guess at his motive, but his alibi had not yet been confirmed. He might have had an opportunity.

Her thoughts were interrupted by Nathan, who entered the room just then. They all looked at each other awkwardly for a moment, and Leigh realized that the tension that formerly existed between the two men now seemed somewhat muted. Perhaps this was because Nathan no longer viewed Richard as a threat. Not now, with Anastasia dead. Of course, as party to Anastasia's estate, he still could contest the will on her behalf, because she was alive at the time of her mother's death. And with Anastasia out of the way, he could claim her share of the inheritance. A far-flung idea but a motive for his killing her nonetheless.

She made a small grimace and decided she didn't want to get involved in a conversation with these two. She turned to Richard, holding out her hand formally. 'If I don't see you then, goodbye, Richard. I'm sorry about what happened.' It was really all she could muster.

He accepted her hand and gave it a shake. Then he nodded as she turned and walked toward the door.

She closed the door slowly, thinking she might be able to catch some of Richard and Nathan's conversation. For a moment, neither spoke. Then she heard a soft tread as Nathan walked toward the center of the room. But their words were muffled. She left the doorway, not wanting to be accused of eavesdropping.

★   ★   ★

Anastasia must have stumbled and fallen, the coroner concluded, hitting her head on the rock as she slid over the edge. The medical examination showed that death had been a result of a blow to the front and side of the head as a result of her fall. Part of her skull was crushed. The case was closed.

The sheriff had turned up no evidence suggesting that Anastasia's death had been anything but an accident. He informed the family that they were free to leave town. Richard was especially anxious to get away from this place, which represented only death for him.

But the case wasn't satisfactorily closed to Braden's way of thinking. He and Leigh sat in the library mulling over the grim affair. She looked at Braden, who sat with hands folded under his chin, elbows resting on the desk. He stared soberly at the fireplace. Still empty, Leigh noted. On the mantel, the old-fashioned clock ticked in its glass case. Hawthorne's portrait dominated the room, even in the dim light. The big house was quiet. Claudia was leaving tomorrow. Leigh would be left there with Nathan and Hania.

Leigh wasn't sure exactly why she was staying but she felt as if she couldn't just walk off and leave things as they were. Also, there was Braden. Half-formed thoughts tugged at her mind. She wanted to know him better, and he her. Did they have a future?

'You're right,' she said, pulling her mind back to the present conversation with an effort. 'It's too neat. Too pat. There are too many questions unanswered.'

Braden drummed his fingers thoughtfully

on the desk, a habit he seemed to share with Richard, Leigh thought irrelevantly.

'Sheriff McElroy and the coroner were awfully quick to assume accidental death.' He exhaled. 'I've seen or heard of this once too often. A puzzling crime in a small town, and the authorities can't be bothered with it. I don't know if it's because they're not equipped to deal with complexities or are too busy issuing parking tickets.'

'Do you suppose anyone has a reason to hush it up?' she asked.

He shrugged. 'I don't know. But I do know they haven't found all the clues.'

The way he said it made her wary. 'What do you mean?'

'I'm not ready to give it up yet. There are a few things I'd like to investigate myself.'

'Then you don't believe it was just an accident.'

He gave a half snort. 'Does anybody?'

'Well the coroner . . . '

'I'm not talking about the official record.'

He was right. The same thoughts plagued her. 'But we can't just ask Sheriff McElroy to reopen the case on suspicion. We have to have some facts.'

'Exactly.'

'What if Richard and Anastasia were involved in some sort of intrigue?' she asked.

'What if her death has larger implications than what we've seen? Remember, when we went to Richard that night, he said, 'I told her . . .' But he didn't finish his sentence.'

Braden nodded. 'But we reported that to Sheriff McElroy. When he questioned Richard, Richard didn't remember saying that. In fact he didn't even remember what he'd been thinking at the time. Only that he was overwhelmed with shock.'

Braden seemed to discount Leigh's idea of a larger plot. 'It doesn't fit,' he said. 'Her death looked suspicious. A professional killer or someone who had at least brushed shoulders with violence wouldn't have made such a sloppy job of it. If she'd been murdered by someone in criminal circles, the killer would either have removed the body or made it look more like a real accident.'

'I suppose,' Leigh said.

'This was definitely the work of an amateur.' His dark hair fell over his brow, and his eyes had a luminous faraway look. His lip twitched every few seconds as if punctuating his thoughts. 'We have to look at it from another angle, Leigh.'

'What angle?'

'I need to ask you some questions.'

'Me?' Her eyes widened.

'About Anastasia. Perhaps you know

something about her relations with other people, the rest of the family.'

'Well, she was not well liked, at least by the people here. But you could see that. She's always been aggressive and jealous, and she always sought attention.' Leigh shook her head. 'It's too bad. She must have tried to substitute attention for love. Hmmm, that's funny.'

It brought her back to her earlier thought that Anastasia had sought attention especially from their father. She said as much to Braden. 'There was something similar in Anastasia's personality and Father's. They were both daring and outspoken, couldn't be bothered with details. 'As if' — she gestured with her hand — 'they were painted in broad strokes.' She smiled slightly.

Braden nodded attentively. 'Go on.'

'Odd how much Anastasia was like Father, though she had mother's features,' said Leigh. 'She had none of Sybil's stern quietness. There was nothing reserved about her, if you know what I mean. And yet Anastasia wasn't Hawthorne's favorite, she was Mother's. She always knew how to please Mother while at the same time getting her own way.'

'And from what you've said, Hawthorne was Hania's protector,' Braden said. He leaned back in the leather chair. 'It doesn't make sense on the surface of things, but there's never a crime without a motive. There's something missing, something vital that we don't know. It's the only explanation for this whole mess.'

'It would make more sense if someone who was angry over the unequal inheritance attempted to harm or frighten Hania,' Leigh said. 'In fact, maybe they tried, only they mistook Anastasia for Hania?' It wasn't likely, but she was grasping at straws.

'Except they don't look anything alike.'

'No, of course not. I look more like Anastasia than Hania does.'

Braden studied her features. 'You know you're right. With heavier makeup . . . ' he didn't finish his sentence.

She went on. 'And according to Doc Thomas, it was daylight. But what would Hania or Anastasia or any of us be doing at the mine, especially dressed like she was?'

'She might have gone there to meet someone.'

Leigh furrowed her brow. It was the first idea that held any possibility. 'But assuming someone asked Anastasia to go there, what did he or she want?'

'I'm not sure,' Braden said slowly. 'But perhaps we're getting somewhere. For the moment, let's leave open the question of why someone would want to harm either Hania or Anastasia. Let's talk about something else. Let's go back to the will.'

Leigh clasped her hands around one lifted knee. 'You still think the accident had something to do with that?'

'Cause and effect. The timing was right.'

Something about his hypothesis still bothered her, though she couldn't put her finger on what it was.

'Now, you knew Sybil better that I did,' he said. 'Why would she leave everything to Hania?'

Leigh shook her head. 'I've tried to figure that out. I don't know.'

'When was Hania born?' Braden asked.

'Well, she's forty-six. Her birthday's in February.'

'And Anastasia. How much younger is she?'

'Sixteen years. You see, Mother and Father moved here after Hania was born. Then Father was in the war, and Anastasia didn't come along for some time after that.'

Braden leaned forward. 'So Hania wasn't born here?'

'No, why?'

'I'm not sure. It may not mean anything. But we're speculating. Could there have been something that happened in Denver all those years ago that made Sybil leave everything to Hania?'

Leigh cocked her head. 'I never thought of that. I suppose it's possible.'

Braden scratched his temple. 'My father might know. I think he met the family when they moved here.'

'It's worth a try.'

'Yes. He might remember something that happened between Sybil and Hawthorne upon the birth of their first child, perhaps a promise of some kind.'

'You mean something he hasn't told you.'

Braden nodded. 'Yes. Something he had no reason to tell me, but that might have a correlation. I'll ask him this evening.'

'Oh, wait a minute. There is something I'd forgotten. My father came here with a cousin; Charlie was his name. They went into the copper-mining business together. They also bought land. But later there was a feud. I didn't see much of Charlie as I was growing up. By that time, he had sold his part of the business to Father and moved away.'

'Now that you've got me thinking,' she said, 'I suppose there could be some sort of family secret.' She looked at him intently, her heartbeat quickening.

'What if Hania is illegitimate? Maybe my mother was making up for some sort of wrong she had done. It sounds incredible, I know, but,' she shrugged, 'we have to try something.'

'No one has ever said anything to that effect, have they?'

'Never. There was never a reason to think anything of the kind. Besides, if Hania was born out of wedlock, why would Hawthorne care for her so much? Besides, single women didn't keep their illegitimate children in those days — not in 1941. Sybil would have given her up for adoption.'

'Unless Sybil married soon after she became pregnant and deceived Hawthorne about the birth,' he said.

'Maybe. Of course, I never would have known if something like that happened. None of us would. Do you want to ask Hania?'

'Eventually, yes, but as you say, she might not know. There's another way.'

'Birth records.'

'I'd like to take a look at all of your birth certificates. Do you know where they are?'

Leigh thought. It had been years since she'd had any reason to wonder where family documents of that kind were kept. 'There's a metal box in the attic, I believe. It's been there since my father died. They might be inside.'

'Good. Is it locked?'

'There might be a key. Look in the desk drawer there. I think I remember seeing a ring of keys.' She also remembered Richard looking for stationery in the desk the night she'd accidentally encountered him. Was it just coincidence?

She came around behind Braden and helped him rummage in the drawer. As she had suspected, there was an old rusty key ring with several tarnished keys on it. She lifted it out.

'Here it is.'

'If you're right then, one of these keys will fit the box.'

'I think so,' she said.

'Good. Then we'll go to the attic this evening. In the meantine, I think I'll have a talk with my father. He may remember things he hasn't thought of before.'

Braden stood, touching Leigh's hair with his right hand. 'Will you have dinner with me?' he asked quietly. 'Then we can explore the attic together.'

She gave him a wry smile. 'In the moonlight. Of course, I may have to protect you from the ghost.'

He gave her a puzzled look. 'What ghost?'

Half seriously she said, 'Sybil, I would suppose, if there is one. Unless Hawthorne is still hanging around thumping out messages.'

'One knock for yes, two for no?'

'I don't think there's really a ghost. But I did hear a — and feel — something the night I got home.'

'Oh?'

'Yes. It was scary at first. I thought maybe Mother's spirit was trying to tell me something. Later I heard something or someone in the attic.'

'I wonder,' Braden said.

She got his meaning. 'You mean it was probably a more earthly visitor? Whoever it was might have been looking for the same documents we're looking for now?'

'If so, we're on the right track.'

For a moment, they gazed at each other, and Leigh longed to move toward him. But she fought the feeling, and by his look, she thought he did likewise. They were partners in this grisly investigation but no more until matters were solved.

With an effort, she moved away. If only they could forget everything. If only he would put his arms around her and hold her. But she fought the fantasy.

He hesitated for a moment, sensing her need. 'Leigh,' he murmured softly.

'I know,' she said tentatively, touching his lapel.

'It's important to me that you be satisfied

about your mother's will. I want you to believe that my father had nothing to do with her decision to revise the will.'

'I know that.'

'And that I know nothing I haven't told you.'

At the mention of the will, Leigh sighed. He was right. He could satisfy her feminine instincts, but nothing would satisfy her mind until she found some answers to the puzzle that was her family.

She turned away, her face flushed. 'Dinner then,' she said.

'Be ready at seven. 'We'll eat at the steak-house, and I'll let you know what my father said.'

'I could go with you to question your father.'

'No, he might be inhibited by your presence. If he remembers anything, I'll get his agreement that I can repeat it to you. If he has some reason to keep it secret, I'll let you know why I can't tell you. All right?'

'All right.'

She walked him to the door. Dinner at the steakhouse would be fine. It was too gloomy and lonely to eat in this house anymore.

[Journal Entry]   **November 16, 1939**

Father passed away two nights ago. I couldn't bear it. I sat holding his hand in the dark until they made me come away. I couldn't cry. I didn't know what to do. Finally the priest took me home.

I didn't want to see anybody. Hawthorne came to pay his respects. He and Charlie were at the funeral, only I didn't want to see them afterward.

— S.P.

10

Leigh stood before the door to her mother's room. She held her breath as she put her hand on the polished-brass doorknob. The door opened smoothly, and she realized someone must have oiled the hinges so that Sybil would not be disturbed when servants, doctors, or family came in and out.

She shut the door behind her and let out her breath. She had not come here since she'd been home, but she knew it would be better to confront the room than to avoid it indefinitely. There was the possibility that Sybil had left a clue here, and if so, Leigh was determined to find it.

The huge four-poster, upholstered in dark red, dominated the room. It faced a Chinese Chippendale mirror, which hung over a white marble fireplace, and was flanked by two pagoda bedside tables. The willow-pattern fabric of the drapes was repeated on the wall covering. Deep reds and golds were carried out in the Chinese screen that stood before the fireplace, the upholstered mahogany chairs, the two cinnabar vases, and the rose bowl that adorned the mantelpiece.

The drapes were pulled over the windows, and the bed was freshly made. Leigh could see that Mrs. Garcia must have had the maids do everything possible to make the room seem fresh and clean, though Leigh suspected guests would not use it for some time.

Leigh remembered the feeling that her mother's presence had drifted through her bedroom the night she arrived, and she waited a second as she stood in the center of the room to see if she sensed anything here now. But there was no feeling of another presence. Her mother's spirit had truly fled.

Leigh half smiled to herself. She must have been hoping that if Sybil were still haunting them, she could guide Leigh to a clue. But then that was improbable. Sybil's ghost would probably be as secretive as Sybil had been when she was alive.

She began an inspection of the room, hoping she might find old letters, a diary, anything that might have documented intentions. Sybil was evidently of sound mind and knew what she was doing. She might have left her thoughts about the will somewhere in writing, perhaps even unconsciously.

On the surface, Anastasia's death seemed unrelated. Except that Leigh had a feeling, deep within her, that there was some connection, though she didn't know what. It seemed logical to her that if they could understand the circumstances leading up to the drafting of the will, that might enable them to understand how Anastasia died.

She heard voices in the hall and instinctively moved behind the door. She wasn't really afraid of being caught, but if she was going to search her mother's room, she would rather do it privately. It was hard to admit she felt that way, because she was not yet certain who the guilty parties might be.

The voices passed. Leigh moved to the small writing desk next to the window and sat in the chair. The top pulled down to create a writing surface. Envelopes and papers were stuffed neatly into cubbyholes and slots. A small drawer in the center slid open to reveal rubber bands, erasers, paper clips, a small metal ruler, pens, and an old-fashioned bottle of ink.

Three small keys lay in the drawer, and Leigh lifted them out. One of them seemed to fit the drawer beneath the writing surface, which she lifted up again and shut to be able to open the drawer.

The small key turned in the lock, and the drawer slid open. In it were boxes of stationery, Christmas cards with the Castle name engraved in gold, several pads of lined paper, and an envelope of receipts. She examined the receipts. They were from local vendors and were mostly for household items and kitchen supplies.

But there was nothing more personal than that in the drawer. Why then had it been locked? She shut the drawer and studied it. She'd heard of false bottoms and wondered if this desk harbored one. She examined the height of the drawer and opened it again, lifting out some of the boxes and reaching down with her fingers. But there was nothing obvious about it. The bottom of the drawer seemed solid.

She frowned in concentration. The smaller drawers in the top of the desk all slid open easily, revealing nothing more interesting than check-books, bank statements, more household receipts, and another dried-up bottle of ink. She felt around the edges of the desk, but there were no secret springs or panels that gave way.

She gazed about the rest of the room. If Sybil had left any personal letters lying about, they had to be somewhere, though they might not necessarily be in this room. Still, that drawer had been locked. Why? Perhaps for no reason, since the key was so readily available.

She returned to the drawer. This time she lifted out all the contents and stacked everything on the floor. Then she saw what she'd been looking for. The bottom of the desk was hinged at the back. A small crack in the center panel gave away the fact that there was indeed a false bottom.

With growing excitement, Leigh looked for something narrow that would slip into the panel and lift it. She tried pressing the back, and the edge of the panel at the front lifted enough for her to hold it with the tip of her finger. So Sybil had gone to some trouble to provide herself with a place to keep items not meant for other people's eyes!

Leigh grasped the panel more firmly now and pulled it all the way up. It lifted easily, revealing the cavity beneath, which was just wide enough to store papers, folders, or a notebook.

But it was empty.

She stared at the space in disappointment. She'd been so sure there would be something there. She bent to look at the empty drawer more closely. It was clean; only a few traces of dirt were gathered at the edges. But she was unable to tell whether anything had lain there recently.

She exhaled and slumped back in the chair, letting the false bottom drop. The sound made her jump, reminding her that she didn't want to be caught nosing around her mother's personal things. If the wrong person should find her doing so . . . But she put that thought aside and quickly replaced the contents of the drawer before shutting it.

Logic told her that if Sybil had gone to such lengths to have a false bottom constructed, at one time she must have had something to hide there. But then, later on, the drawer no longer served its purpose.

Leigh's eyes roamed to the other objects in the room and finally came to the bed, with its heavy red draperies, its tall canopy, and hanging passementerie bells, making it look like a fantasy pagoda. Sybil had chosen all Chinese decor for this room and had designed it with care. She had spent her last several weeks in that bed, refusing to be committed to a hospital. Leigh stood and walked over to it, then sat down on the thick quilt that covered it. The springs supported her weight easily.

She glanced back at the writing desk and then said to herself, 'Of course.' It was only a few steps from the desk to the bed, but a person who was ill would not have had the strength to reach it. Even before Sybil had become completely bedridden, it must have taken more effort than she could afford, if she wanted to write frequently.

Leigh immediately began to explore the ebony pagoda-like bedside table, with its two shelves, to the right of the bed. The top shelf held a vase of flowers and two ornamented plates. On the bottom shelf were a dozen or so books, neatly stacked. The maids had removed all trace of the medicines or personal items Sybil must have kept there.

Leigh looked at the books first, not daring to hope she might find a letter tucked in between pages. Two novels, several travel books with elaborate color photography, and two oversize home-decorating books revealed no clues.

And there was nothing else on the bedside stand: no concealed drawers or panels that Leigh could see. She walked around the bed. A similar inspection of the matching pagoda-shaped table on the other side yielded nothing either.

Useless, she thought. There didn't seem to be anything at all. She leaned back against the headboard. For a moment, dizziness overcame her as she placed herself in the position her mother must have been in just before her death. When the light-headedness left her, she slid further down in the bed, and then extended her arms to either side to assess the reach possible from the bed. But the only things within reach were the two bedside tables, and she had already checked those.

Then she lifted her arms and grasped the

molding on the curved headboard. It appeared to be solid.

She lowered her arms and rolled over on her stomach, resting her chin on her elbows and staring at the same red quilted fabric that covered the headboard as well as the rest of the bed. Then she saw it. There was a seam on the strip that covered the molding on the right, but on the left, the seam stopped partway down the S-shaped curve that led to the bed frame. On the lower portion, there was no seam. Rather, there was a thin line where the material seemed to be tucked around the board.

She ran her finger along it, tracing the shallow S curve to the end of the board. It almost looked as if the molding could be removed. She examined the other side. Here, tiny threads were visible in a stitch that simply outlined the molding, nothing else.

Her heartbeat quickened. The two sides of a piece that ought to be symmetrical were not the same. She sat up now, so as to better examine the side that seemed unusual. Material tucked around a board that way might indicate an opening. The quilted padding prevented her from ascertaining if the headboard was hollow. By pressing around the bottom of the headboard, she found what she'd been looking for. There was a slight indentation at the bottom, and she pressed inward. As she did so, she felt the panel give. It moved in a good two inches.

As she bent forward, her eyes widened. Slipped down into the crevice, was a thick book, bound in calfskin. The moment her fingers touched it, she knew she had a find. She pulled the book out and let the panel fall back into place.

Then she froze. Someone was coming along the hallway. Quickly she slid the book under the pillow and jumped up.

Whoever it was paused in front of the door. Leigh tried to swallow, but her throat was dry. Should she walk over and open the door, or just wait here until he or she decided to go on or enter? And what kind of explanation would she give if someone came in?

She tried to tell herself it was ridiculous to feel this way. Why shouldn't she have come to her mother's room? If only her face didn't feel so hot, and she could breathe normally.

The person outside the door waited for several seconds. Then as if he had had a change of heart, he retraced his steps. She could hear a light footstep on the stair at the end of the hall and knew the person had gone down.

Leigh breathed easier. She walked to the window and pulled back the drapes. She wanted to re-establish a sense of normalcy before she went on with her search. That way if someone did see her here, she could say something coherent.

When she had herself under control, she returned to the bed, extracted the book and took a seat in the wing chair next to the window. It was a bound volume of lined sheets, gilt at the edges.

From the small, tight handwriting that filled every page, she could see that it was her mother's diary. She turned to the front and noted that the date of the first entry was the summer before last. So there must be earlier volumes somewhere, she thought, unless Sybil had only then begun to keep the journal.

She read the first few pages with interest, though the topics mentioned held no real significance for her. There was a description of an outing Sybil had gone on with friends and some comments on the upcoming marriage of a neighbor's daughter. Then a few pages turned more introspective, and to Leigh, they were confusing.

The pages spoke of an empty house and loneliness. They betrayed a bitter outlook. There were references to Cousin Charlie and how something was his fault. There were pages where Sybil seemed to be reviewing her

191

life and asking herself if she had done the right thing.

Leigh shook her head, a feeling of desolation creeping over her. Then she shut the book and got to her feet. If she were going to study the diary, as she knew she must, she would have to do it elsewhere, not here, where her mother's joys and sorrows overwhelmed her at every turn.

She crossed the room and opened the door a crack. There was no one in the hall. She slipped out, shutting the door softly. Then she hurried to the east wing, where she could read undisturbed in her room.

[Journal Entry]   **January 20, 1940**

Hawthorne and I were married yesterday morning. There was little else to do. He wants to take charge of my life, so I let him.

I don't love him though. How could I? I am still grieving the loss of dear Daddy. I didn't want my husband on my wedding night. I cried, and he was angry, but he left me alone. I cannot tell you how awful this makes me feel. That part of me is sacred, and I didn't want to give it lightly. It is the last thing I have left of myself.

— S.C.

11

Leigh read through the entire journal, and when she had finished, she was more puzzled than when she had begun. In recent years, Sybil had mixed the past and present together so that it was hard for Leigh to unscramble her meaning. It could mean that Sybil had turned senile in her last year. She could also have done this on purpose, to confuse the reader. But then, she had not meant for anyone else to read this. Or had she?

In many places, Sybil had used an initial or a pronoun instead of a full name, so that it was unclear who she was writing about.

There were more puzzling references to Hawthorne's cousin Charlie and notations stating that she really held no grudge against H. He had been merely trying to help.

The last entry, dated November 10, only eight days before she died, was the most mysterious:

Life ebbs from me. Those who have gone before me await me. Do they know what is in my heart? These last nine years, I have questioned much, wondering if God will

194

take his vengeance from me. I leave it in His hands. If I am an instrument of His will, then matters will take their course as I think they should.

If He is angry with me, then earthly atonement will be done, and God will stay her hand — my daughter who knows her heritage, for have I not bred her in my footsteps?

I can surely rest easy, for the Lord knows how I have suffered. My last gesture carries with it the irony that life has forced upon us.

My only doubt, and I confess it here in my journal, in what must surely be my last entry — for how can I expect another good day while this illness claims more and more of me — my only doubt is that there is one other who knows my secret. I had meant to tell A. of it, but I do not expect her to arrive in time. And can I trust a letter? I think not. For other eyes could peruse a letter not meant for them. I must leave it in her hands, trusting she will know how to remove all obstacles. The other two may wonder, but they will benefit in the end, for are not three parts larger each than if divided by four?

I tire even as I write, and I must stop. I will put away this journal where I have shared so many thoughts known to no other. My body will soon turn to dust, and so will these pages. But no matter, for what's done is done.

What was she talking about? A. must stand for Anastasia. What had she wanted to tell her? Most of all, what were the three parts and the four?

The entry strengthened Leigh's resolve to search for earlier volumes of the diary, for perhaps they would clarify the meaning of this passage. Sybil made mention of questioning herself these last nine years. That could only mean one thing: that she had changed her will nine years ago. The explanation for her action must be in the diary that covered that period. But where were such volumes?

Leigh returned to her mother's bedroom and sat on the bed again. She slipped the headboard section back and looked more closely at the hiding place. But there was nothing else there. She let the panel fall back into place and shook her head. She felt suddenly tired and longed for a nap. But she wanted to get as much done as possible before she saw Braden again at seven. That gave her an hour.

On impulse, she decided to check her father's old study for any family documents that might be in there. The study was in the west wing, which was seldom used now. Many of the rooms in that wing had been closed off.

Before she could go there, though, she remembered she had to let Mrs. Garcia know she wouldn't be dining at home that evening. So she returned the diary to its hiding place and went downstairs. After exchanging a few words with the loyal domestic, she mounted the back stairs to the west wing. The stairs had not been used much since the family had let most of the servants go. Now it was just Mrs. Garcia, the upstairs maids and Carlos.

She paused on the second-floor landing that opened to the west wing. She looked up the flight that led to a third floor of servants' quarters, which connected with the attic she and Braden were planning to visit later that evening. It had been years since she'd visited the servants' quarters, where Mrs. Garcia and Carlos still had rooms. No need to invade their privacy now, she thought as she left the landing and passed through a door to a hallway much like the one where her own bedroom was.

Here the carpet looked faded. It must have been some time since it was cleaned. She turned the rheostat on the wall, but no lights came on overhead. Evidently no one had bothered to replace light bulbs, since these rooms were no longer in use.

It was easy to remember the days when guests came and went here and the chandeliers gleamed with their electric lights. She paused to try a doorknob, and to her surprise, the door opened easily. At first she did not know where she was, for the furniture was covered with dust covers, and there were no pictures on the wall. All the rooms had once held paintings or reproductions, and it was from those that she had first developed her interest in art. She could remember sitting in the various rooms of the houses, a sketch pad in her lap, copying the pictures on the walls. And her mother had encouraged her.

Now, standing in this room, she tried to remember what it had been used for, and what pictures had hung here. She stepped closer to the walls — pale blue, now gray with dust. She raised her hand to touch a spot that was lighter than the rest of the wall, then ran her finger downward. There was a line where a picture had been taken down fairly recently, for around it, the dust was thicker.

She studied the other aspects of the room. It was a sitting room with an adjoining door. Two brass candle holders, corroded now, jutted from the walls. She thought she remembered a large oil painting hanging between them. The adjoining door led to a bedroom, but there the artwork remained. She cocked her head and studied the Spanish soldier with his shield.

This must have been a guest room. No one had lived here on a regular basis. But in the days when guests were frequent, and the aunts had come down from Denver, she thought they had stayed here.

Sunlight was held at bay by grimy curtains. A braided rug covered the hardwood floor that had long since lost its luster. She returned to the sitting room. Closing her eyes, she tried to recall the room with the pictures still on the walls, but it just wouldn't come. So she decided to move on.

Out of curiosity, she decided to look at the other rooms as well before seeking out the study. Most of the bedrooms were much the same: shrouded furniture and dusty curtains. She noticed that the art had been taken down in only one other room. Of course it would make sense that Sybil had moved the paintings to a more prominent place when this wing fell into disuse. She tried to remember if there was an inventory of artwork. There must be one among the papers having to do with the estate. By checking the list, she could determine which paintings were missing, and perhaps she could discover why a few of them had been moved — or sold.

But it seemed a monumental task to run such a check on the artwork, and for what purpose? It might lead nowhere. She shook her head, feeling the frustration of being cast into the role of sleuth.

Suddenly she stiffened. From down the hall, a door creaked. She turned to face the sound. The old house was full of sounds, and there might even be a stray cat or mouse about in a wing that was no longer used. But she had the distinct feeling that a person had opened a door.

Her heart pounded in her chest even as she told herself she was foolish to be frightened.

Moving forward, she decided it was wiser to confront whoever it was in the hallway, rather than be trapped in this room. She moved quickly to the door, which she had left ajar. Stepping around it, she came face to face with Nathan, who had his hand on the doorknob of the room from which Leigh had noticed the art had been removed.

From the look on his face, he was as shocked to meet her as she was him, and he snatched his hand from the door as if caught in a guilty act. Leigh stared at him, her heart still pounding in her throat. She did not know what she had expected, but she had certainly not expected him. And yet, why not? After all, he was master of this house now. He must be curious as to what he owned.

Then she thought of another possibility. What if Nathan had killed Anastasia because he knew she planned to contest the will? Couldn't he have taken steps to ensure there would be no trouble from Anastasia?

An even more horrible thought followed. The will stated that if Hania didn't survive, the other three sisters would split the inheritance — the 'three parts' would be more than the 'four.' If Nathan had expected Anastasia to make an attempt on her older sister's life, was it possible that Nathan had put her out of the way to prevent it?

Leigh trembled. What if she was facing Anastasia's killer? And what if he decided to do away with her as well for snooping around? She tried to control her runaway emotions. Surely he would not harm her in this very house. It would be too obvious. Surely, and yet . . .

'Nathan,' she finally said, realizing she had been staring at him for an inordinate amount of time.

'I didn't expect to find anyone up here,' he said, taking several steps toward her.

Involuntarily she backed away, then forced

herself to stop. She mustn't appear frightened.

'Nor did I,' she said.

For a moment they just looked at each other, and Leigh was about to explain what she was doing. But she needed to be on the offensive, not the defensive.

'It's a long time since these rooms were used,' she chatted.

He brushed some imaginary dust from his hands. 'Were you looking for something?'

Did his tone hold an element of menace, or was it just her imagination?

'No, just exploring. We girls used to run about this wing when we were younger.'

He gave her a deprecating glance. 'Indeed.' Then trying a door, though not the one he had first been about to open, he said, 'I thought I'd have a look about — see what use these rooms might be put to.'

She wanted to laugh, but was afraid it was the laughter of hysteria rather than humor. 'Do you have plans for them?'

'Perhaps,' he said seriously. 'I can't see just letting a mansion like this sit empty. I, that is, we are considering some renovation, then a business venture of some sort.'

'I see.' Could he mean they would rent apartments or make the place into a restaurant? Her instincts rebelled against it,

202

but realistically she knew that many homes such as this had been made over in just such a manner. It was too expensive to keep them up otherwise.

He expounded on his thoughts as he examined the ceilings, the flocking on the walls. 'Yes, it has possibilities.'

She could see the dollars stacking in his mind. Of course he would want to turn the house to a profit. Being a banker, he had a natural affinity for money, and apparently some of his other ventures had not gone as planned. Was he desperate enough to kill for it? she wondered. A gleam came into his eyes as he turned to Leigh.

'May I ask what you wished to accomplish by your explorations? Just indulging in a bit of nostalgia?' Again the gleam, the menace — but then she was afraid she was becoming paranoid. She tossed her hair over her right shoulder.

'Yes, if you must know. I was just remembering some things.' She looked him directly in the eye. *Braden Lancaster doesn't think Anastasia's death was an accident,* she wanted to say. *You wouldn't venture an opinion, would you?* But she knew it was pointless. Either way he would say he didn't know what she was talking about.

His eyes squinted, and his face seemed to

tighten. He let it drift off, but she noticed his right hand go into his pocket and grip something. As he looked at her, she tried to read what was in his face — avarice, jealousy, guilt? Or just plain evil? It was not a pleasant face.

Her fear had abated somewhat, but she knew it would be futile to stay here. Whatever he had come to do, he would not do while she remained.

'If you don't mind,' she said. 'I'd like to sit in the study for a while.'

'Surely the library downstairs . . . ,' he said.

She shook her head. 'I always kept my favorite books up here. Father used to transact personal business in the upstairs study, and he would let me sit there and read. If you don't mind, that is.' She looked at him politely, forcing him to agree unless he really wanted to appear domineering.

'Very well. Please see that you don't disturb anything else.'

She clenched her teeth. She wanted to yell at him — order him out of her house, the house where she had grown up. But she managed to remain silent and to walk sedately to the opposite end of the hallway, near the landing that led to the bedrooms they were currently using. She opened the door to the upstairs study and went in. This room, unlike the other rooms, had more recently seen use. The roll-top desk was closed and locked, she found, but the chairs had recently been dusted. Shelves ran around three sides of the room. She flicked a finger against a tassle hanging from a lamp shade and felt the back of the smooth oak armchair.

The desk might be locked, but it was not impenetrable. She smiled to herself as she pressed the spring in the molding at the side of the desk and the lock slipped back. She touched the desk top and then thought of Nathan. If he caught her rummaging around in the desk, he would surely make a scene — or even worse. She had not forgotten that he was, perhaps, the most likely suspect for Anastasia's murderer.

No, she wouldn't take the chance. But later she could come back here with Braden or Claudia. Two against one seemed somehow safer.

She was about to leave when something caught her eye. It was a plaque on the wall that had been engraved in bronze. Castle & Castle Copper Mining Company. It made her think of Cousin Charlie, Hawthorne's partner in the early days, who was dead now. But Sybil had made mention of him in her diary. It had been a long time ago when Leigh last saw him, and she never knew him very well.

In fact she couldn't really remember what he looked like.

She stared at the plaque for some time. Her father had had it made to commemorate their tenth year in business. Leigh must have been about seven, she thought. Hawthorne was always more active in the business than his second cousin. Charlie eventually went back to Denver, and there he'd passed away. But Hawthorne had never bought him out, to Leigh's knowledge.

She frowned at the plaque. All that must have been settled years ago. She assumed that Charlie's shares in the business must have gone to his heirs, whoever they were.

She fingered the tarnished copper. She had half a mind to take it down and have it polished, but she knew she dared not remove anything. Approaching footsteps reminded her of Nathan's presence, and she walked to the center of the room, not wanting him to see her touching the plaque.

The door creaked as he pushed it open with his hand.

'I was just going,' she said and moved to pass him. He stood aside, watching her walk to the landing, across which she opened the door that led to the bedrooms.

Then he entered the study.

★ ★ ★

As Leigh went along to her bedroom, she remembered what it was that had started her thinking. Seeing the plaque had jarred her memory. When Cousin Charlie had come to visit, he had stayed in the far guest room as well — the one with the missing art.

'Hi, sis.' Claudia emerged from her room and shut the door behind her.

'Oh, hello, Claudia.' Leigh smiled ruefully.

'Sorry if I scared you. You seem jumpy.'

'I guess I am a little. I was having a look at the old wing.'

'Really?' Claudia's interest was piqued. 'Anything interesting?'

'Well, as a matter of fact, yes.' Leigh looked toward her room. 'Let's sit down.'

In her bedroom, the women took seats in the easy chairs on opposite sides of the window. Leigh threw her shoes off and tucked her feet under her. When she was settled, she said. 'You remember Cousin Charlie?'

Claudia creased her brow. 'Vaguely. Daddy's partner, you mean?'

'That's right. They were still partners till the end, weren't they? I mean until the mines were sold and Father retired, turning over the management to Mr. Hardgood.'

'Yes, I remember that. It was just before

207

Dad died.' Claudia gave Leigh a look. 'No one in the family's been involved in the management of the company or the property since then. I suppose Nathan will change all that.'

'I suppose, even though the mine isn't nearly as active as it used to be. Did Charlie have any children?'

Claudia shook her head. 'Wasn't married. In fact, I think that's why he left here. I think he and Daddy argued. Besides, Charlie was a bachelor, and there wasn't much for a bachelor to do in a small town like this. Denver was more to his liking. I don't think Mother was sad to see him go either. What made you think of him?'

'I was in the upstairs study, and the plaque on the wall reminded me.'

'Oh, yes, the one they had made to celebrate the tenth anniversary of the company.'

'Yes. You were awfully young then, how do you remember?'

Claudia smiled thoughtfully. 'Actually, I don't. But Mother used to speak of it. Like I said, I had the feeling she didn't like Charlie. She didn't like his wild ways.'

'But she put up with him because he was Father's partner?'

'Something like that. He used to stay in

one of the guest rooms after he moved back to Denver and visited here on business. I remember seeing him a few times then.'

'Yes, I think you're right,' said Leigh.

'He looked a lot like Daddy, I always thought. But they were only second cousins.'

Leigh shook her head. 'You've a better memory than I have.'

'Oh, he was tall, but more slender than Dad, and his hair was darker. But he had that same brightness in the eyes and that same square chin. I liked him even if Mother didn't.

'Look, Leigh,' said Claudia, gazing directly at her sister. 'I know you're not satisfied with the way things stand around here' — she grimaced — 'Anastasia and other things.'

Leigh nodded. 'Braden seems to think she was murdered, and I think I agree.'

Claudia shifted in her seat and looked out the window. 'I wouldn't be surprised.'

'Why?'

She looked at Leigh again. 'Anastasia didn't have very many friends.'

'No, she didn't. But, Claudia, do you think her murder, if it was that, was connected in any way to Mother's will?'

'How could it be? I would more easily conceive of Anastasia killing someone to get her hands on the money.'

The same thought they all had. Then aloud, Leigh said, 'I wonder if she tried.'

'What?'

'Oh, nothing. It is odd that she died, that's all.'

Claudia gave a small shudder. 'If anyone killed her, he certainly did a thorough job of covering his tracks.'

Leigh stretched her legs out in front of her and pondered the bits and pieces of the case. 'Oh, Claudia, there is one more thing. In the room Charlie and the aunts used to use, two pictures have been taken down. Do you know where they might be?'

'Haven't the foggiest. Why?'

'It may not mean anything, but it bugs me that I can't remember what they looked like.'

'Hmm. There are a lot of pictures in this house. I suppose Mother might have sold some.'

'She might have. But why those and not the rest? Only one other is missing on that floor that I can tell.'

'Maybe somebody liked them. Maybe they were all by the same artist or something.'

'Or of the same person,' Leigh murmured almost to herself.

Claudia stared at her for a moment, then frowned. 'Leigh, if you don't mind my saying so, I think maybe you're letting your imagination run away with you a little. You ought not to spend so much time alone here.'

Leigh smirked. 'I suppose you're right. I keep hoping for a clue.'

'Well,' Claudia said with a sigh as she got up. 'If you keep digging, I suppose you might find one. Only do me a favor.'

'What?'

'Be careful.'

12

'He said that Sybil never talked about that period in Denver when she and Hawthorne were young,' Braden said. 'Funny, he didn't seem to want to talk about it himself.' Leigh and Braden were sitting at the steakhouse, at a small table with a red check tablecloth spread under platters of sizzling sirloins.

'Do you think he could have been hiding something?' Leigh asked.

Braden chewed a mouthful of steak before continuing. 'I never would have thought he'd have anything to hide, but I wonder.' He frowned, jabbing a fork into his salad bowl.

'Did you tell him we were looking for the birth certificates?' she asked.

'I did. That's when he seemed nervous to me.'

'How do you mean?'

'I can't explain. It's just a feeling I got. I know him pretty well.'

'Of course.' They ate in silence for a moment.

'We should clear it with your other sisters before we go looking,' he said.

'Well, it's not illegal if I go to the attic in

my own . . . ' She stopped. It was no longer her attic. She put her elbows on the table, clasping her hands over her plate. She sighed. 'I keep forgetting. You're right. We'll ask Hania.'

She told him about the diary and her run-in with Nathan, and he listened thoughtfully.

'This Cousin Charlie,' he said when she had finished, 'how does he fit in?'

She shrugged. 'I never knew him very well. After he moved to Denver, he only came down on occasional business trips. I got the feeling Mother never liked him. I asked Claudia if she thought he had any heirs.'

Braden shook his head. 'If you mean would Charlie's relatives be able to contest the will, the answer is no. Everything was in Sybil's name after Hawthorne died. I'm sure of that.'

Leigh frowned in concentration. 'You know that bothers me about Mother. I'm beginning to see that she had a great many secrets, probably a great many dislikes. And yet she never confided in any of us.' Leigh shook her head. 'It's odd to think she kept so many things from us, and I don't know why.'

Braden moved his hand nearer hers on the table. 'I'm sorry if it's upsetting to you.'

'Not upsetting exactly. I was never one for

213

pity or sympathy — but unsettling. There's a difference.'

'I know,' he said.

They finished the rest of the meal in silence, and Leigh observed him when he wasn't looking. She was beginning to memorize the details of his face, from the small scar to his dark brows, high temples, and the slight cleft in his chin. When she looked at him, a chord was struck in her, causing a flush to come to her face. How she would like for him to tell her to forget their concern for the birth certificates, to suggest they return for a quiet evening at his house. She remembered the feel of his arms around her, and the heat started to build within her.

Self-consciously, she looked up to find him staring at her, and the look in his eye told her he read her thoughts.

'Oh,' she said before she realized she had spoken aloud.

Then a slow smile began at his lips and reached his eyes. He signaled the waiter for the check while she fumbled with her napkin.

As they stood, he reached for her and guided her out the door. Leigh caught a few smiles of people they passed. *Is it that obvious?* she wondered. She felt like she must be wearing a sign that advertised her feelings.

But Braden seemed unruffled. At the car,

he paused before opening her door. His hand slipped around her waist, and his lips brushed her forehead. She instinctively reached for him, forgetting her earlier resolve not to let her feelings interfere with the questions she felt she must settle. Braden pulled her to him slowly and tilted her head back. He kissed her lightly and then opened the door.

It was a good thing to put her in the car like that, she thought with embarrassment. She was afraid she might have made a spectacle of herself in the parking lot. Then she allowed herself a small joke. *What would the neighbors think?*

Ten minutes later they passed through the iron gates and Braden swung the Volvo around the drive. Inside, they found Hania and Nathan having coffee in the dining room with Claudia. Mrs. Garcia was clearing the table. They all stopped talking and looked up as Leigh and Braden entered.

'Hello,' Leigh said as she crossed to them. 'Braden and I are going up to the attic. There are some old family documents up there he's asked to see. I didn't think you'd mind, Hania. I believe the keys to the strongbox are in the desk in the library.' She had rehearsed what she wanted to say, to avoid being stopped by Nathan. But as soon as she'd said it, she thought it must have sounded unnatural.

As Hania looked across the table at Nathan, Leigh tensed. If there was going to be any objection, it was going to come now. Out of the corner of her eye, Leigh saw Claudia shrug as if she didn't care.

Nathan cleared his throat. 'May we know what you are looking for exactly? It's in the attic, you say?'

'Possibly,' said Braden. 'I want to make sure all the family papers are in order, and Leigh thought there might be some in the strongbox that hadn't come to my attention.'

'Look here,' said Nathan, his face reddening slightly. 'If this has anything to do with Hania's inheritance, I think we ought to . . .'

'It's all right,' interrupted Hania in her quiet way. Her voice trembled a little, but she stared rigidly at Nathan. He blustered to a halt. He could hardly argue, since his main opposition was dead. Leigh smiled to herself. For once, Hania was having her way. This was something new.

Hania continued. 'If Braden thinks there may be something of importance in the attic, he should by all means look. Leigh,' she said. 'Take him up, please. There's a flashlight in the pantry.'

She touched the curls around her face in a

nervous manner. Obviously she was not used to crossing her husband. Perhaps her inheritance was giving her a new-found sense of independence. Odd how money affects people, Leigh thought, for she had not stopped to think how it would affect Hania and Nathan. She'd been too busy resenting Nathan's greed.

'Thanks, we'll go up now,' she said, going through the dining room to the kitchen. Braden followed her, shutting the door behind them. Leigh led the way across the kitchen to the pantry and pulled the light string. She spotted the flashlight. Picking it up, she flicked it on, to test the batteries.

'They're dead,' she said when nothing happened. She slid the on-off switch back and forth several times with no result. As she rummaged on the shelf for new ones, Braden asked, 'That night when you thought someone had gone up to the attic — was there a light on?'

She shook her head. 'I didn't see any light. But then I didn't really go up and look. I was at the bottom, in the hallway. Then I went down and found Richard in the library. Well, I guess we'd better ask if there are more batteries somewhere.'

He put a hand out to restrain her. 'Never mind. We don't know that the fixtures upstairs don't work.'

'That's right, we haven't tried them. Follow me then.'

Braden followed her up the back stairs to the second floor. 'There's an entrance to the attic up there,' she said, pointing to the next landing, 'but I don't think it's been used in a long time. We're probably better off using the one in the main wing.'

'Fine,' said Braden.

They went down the darkened corridor Leigh had explored earlier, then entered the main wing of the house. The door to the attic stairway squeaked when she opened it.

'Hang on a second,' she said, feeling her way along. 'The light for the stairway is at the top. That's why I didn't turn it on the night I thought someone was up here.' She shivered a little, remembering her fright.

'An odd construction, isn't it?' Braden said.

'I suppose it is.'

'They might have taken out the light switch down here for some reason,' he said. 'Has anyone ever lived in this attic?'

'Not that I know of.'

They climbed to the landing and Leigh pushed open another door. She located the switch and turned on a light that lighted the stairway and the area round them but left most of the attic still cloaked in darkness.

Leigh walked over the creaking boards to the center of the dusty room and pulled the string attached to an overhead light, but it didn't go on.

'Burned out. Too bad about that flashlight.'

Braden looked up at the moonlight spilling in from the gable windows. 'I think we have enough light for our purpose,' he said, coming to stand near her.

'I hope so. Anyway, I may remember where . . . ' She moved among the boxes, looking over odds and ends of furniture and packing crates. She spotted the large metal box with a lock on the front sitting next to a rusty old filing cabinet.

'I think that's it.' She ran through the keys, trying to remember which one unlocked the metal box. It had been years since she'd seen anybody use it, but the dust seemed lighter on the box top than on the other objects lying near it. She found an old key and tried it.

The lock gave, and the box opened. Manila files were neatly marked with their contents.

'Sybil's handwriting?' said Braden.

'Uh, huh.' She backed away, sneezing from the thick dust surrounding them.

Braden handed her a handkerchief from his pocket, then got down on one knee and read the contents of some of the files. There was a copy of Hawthorne's will and certificate of death.

'Look here.' He stopped suddenly, pulling out a file. 'This one's empty.' He opened it, and Leigh saw there was nothing in it.

'The contents have been taken out recently, I'd say.' He turned the old yellowed file over in his hands. There was no dust inside this file the way there was in the others, suggesting that someone had tampered with it.

Wiping her nose on Braden's handkerchief, Leigh knelt beside him and watched while he went through all the files. The birth certificates were nowhere to be found.

'Not here,' said Leigh. 'I wonder if they ever were.'

He flipped the top of the metal box shut with a loud noise, and the dust flew off it.

'Oh, sorry,' he said, afraid the flying dust would send her into a sneeze attack again. Brushing his fingers through his hair, he said, 'Seems like we've drawn a blank.'

'I'm running out of ideas myself,' she said. 'What shall we do?'

'The hospital should have records,' he said. 'I'll check there. And I'll take this file along to the sheriff. He may be able to get fingerprints from it — if he'll look at it, that is.'

'Right,' she said.

Leigh had gone ahead and was looking at a

cedar chest she remembered as belonging to her mother. She knelt beside it and opened the lid. An alpaca shawl covered the contents.

Then she gasped as she pushed the shawl aside to discover the contents. 'Look,' she said.

There were ten leather volumes similar to the one she had found hidden in her mother's headboard. She lifted one out and opened it. The pages were yellowed and curled at the edges, and the entries were dated ten years earlier.

'What is it?' said Braden, looking over her shoulder.

'The rest of Mother's diaries. Or some of them, at least.'

She handed him the volume and took out the next one. It started where the other one left off.

'Well, there are certainly a lot of them.' She began to pull them out one by one. Though the light was dim, she could see the dates. Her initial enthusiasm for having found the volumes waned as she contemplated reading thousands of pages of the narrow handwriting.

'There seems to be one volume missing,' said Braden. He had glanced at each one as she'd handed it to him. She stood to look. He was right. The last nineteen years of Sybil's life were recorded here, with the exception of one period.

'The year Father died.'

Braden checked the other volumes quickly. 'That year also covered the day she changed her will.'

They stared at each other. 'Where could it be?' she said.

'The question is, has someone else been here before us?' He closed the lid of the cedar chest and answered his own question. 'I'm afraid so. Like on the file, most of the dust has been brushed off.' He pointed to the thick layers of dust and cobwebs that lay everywhere else.

'One of the family?' said Leigh.

'Or Sybil herself?'

'But she was too ill.'

'I'm not so sure. She could get around all right until the last couple of months.'

'That's true. But where would she have put it? I already found the last volume, and there wasn't anything else there, nor in the false-bottom drawer.'

'Well, it might not have been Sybil. It seems obvious that she either had a secret she thought was worth keeping or someone else wanted to hide whatever explanation she might have written down somewhere for changing her will.'

A tremor passed through Leigh, and she gave a short laugh that only punctuated her sense of hopelessness. She couldn't believe that her mother would have gone to such lengths to keep her secrets to herself.

'We can look at them later,' he said, but his tone of voice expressed what she felt — that there would be little point to looking at the volumes that were left. Otherwise, whoever had taken the one special volume would have taken the rest.

'Is there no end?' she asked, and he shook his head, looking up at the skylight dejectedly.

Suddenly Leigh was conscious of his nearness. The magnetism she had felt earlier was still there, but this time her restraint began to disappear. She felt his hand on her waist, then, without planning her reaction, she was in his arms and he kissed her.

As their lips met, his arms went around her and pulled her closer to him until she could feel the beating of his heart, and breathed in his scent.

'Leigh,' he said softly, moving his lips from her face to her ear. His hands gripped her tighter, and she felt the heady sensations she got whenever he held her. She made a small sound in her throat, and he pulled back to look at her face in the shadows. His dark eyes gleamed in the moonlight, questioning her.

'I . . . ' Her voice trailed off. But she took a deep breath and smiled reluctantly, trying to calm her breathing. 'We've still got work to do.'

He nodded and let go of her, glancing around at the odds and ends stored in the attic. Discarded wicker chairs, drooping lamps, boxes of old clothing and books cluttered the space.

'You're right of course.' He struggled with himself for a few moments.

'What else should we look for?' she asked, attempting to get them both back on course.

After a pause, he said, 'What about family albums? Surely your family must have had photos taken. Would they be up here?'

She thought a moment. 'They might be. We did have pictures. I remember Mother sorting through them. Seems like she kept some in a cedar chest about' — she measured with her hands — 'so large.'

He nodded. 'That's what we want. Anything to give us a clue about your sister and your parents' early life.'

'You still believe the answer lies in the past, don't you?'

'I have to think there's an answer and we have to start somewhere,' replied Braden absent-mindedly, running one hand through his hair. 'There haven't been many clues in the present.'

'I suppose you're right.' She wrinkled her nose.

They searched among the boxes for anything that resembled a scrapbook or collection of photographs, and Leigh kept her eyes open for anything that resembled a canvas. After uncovering odds and ends from several lifetimes, Leigh's hand fell on the cedar chest she remembered, partially hidden by canvas from an old deck chair.

'Come here Braden. Help me drag this out.' They removed the canvas and pulled out the old chest. It wasn't locked, and after dusting it off, Leigh reached in to pull out a leather album. 'This is it. This is the one I remember.' The binding was worn, and a strap that once fastened the leaves shut was cracked.

They carried the album over to the window and fingered the leaves. The construction paper crumbled under their touch, and as they turned the pages, the years fell away. The girls when they were small, the old house in Denver. The girls in a Christmas pageant in Culver City. In the silvery moonlight, the faces were arresting, mysterious, caught in actions long forgotten.

'Turn back a moment,' Braden said.

'That's Mother and Father,' Leigh said. 'And that's Hania.' She smiled, lost for a moment in memory. 'I even remember that dress.'

'That's Hawthorne?'

'Yes.' She studied the picture. It was hard to judge attractiveness across the years. Certainly his sober expression and the conservative suits men wore thirty years ago evoked an era.

She studied the pictures one by one, remembering the times or what she'd been told about them. 'Here's the living room in the house in Denver. That's one of the maids. Ann, Anna something. Here, this woman by the coffee urn.' She started to turn the page when the gummed corners holding the picture in place came loose and the picture slipped to the floor.

Both of them bent to pick it up at the same time, but Leigh was the first to reach it. It had landed upside down, and when she picked it up, she read the names scrawled on the back, the ink still visible, but spreading, slightly soaked into the photographic paper.

'Sybil and Hawthorne Castle,' she read. 'With Anna Morgan.'

'Who was Anna Morgan?'

'Well, I don't know exactly, but I think she was a maid. It's funny though. I can't think where I heard of her. Maybe I heard Mother or Father mention her name, I don't know. But this . . . ' She turned the picture over.

'What?' Braden asked, peering at the picture intently.

'The writing. I don't recognize it.'

'Oh, no?'

'No. I know my mother's writing, and it's not Father's either.'

'Then who might have written on these pictures?'

They knelt and pulled the adjacent photos loose. But the writing on the back, when it existed, was Sybil's.

Leigh looked at Braden. 'This one's different. I'm sure of it.'

He frowned, reaching for the picture again. 'Interesting.'

It seemed that Anna Morgan must have played an important part in Leigh's parents' lives. Braden dropped the photo album and rose. A broken doll rolled under his heel, and the rusty mechanism inside revved its tiny motor and hiccuped.

'Mama,' it called in the dark.

13

Leigh saw Claudia off at the tiny airport that serviced the county. Claudia looked out the window at the small plane that waited on the tarmac, her hands stuck in her jacket pockets. She pulled a wry face and said, 'I feel bad leaving on such a sour note.'

'Never mind, sis,' said Leigh. 'There's nothing you can do.'

'I hope you'll be all right.'

They stood still, looking out at the jagged blue mountains in the distance. Close by, brown mesas rose out of the level valley floor where the planes landed.

Leigh turned to Claudia and tried to smile. 'There's nothing to be not all right about. Don't worry. Except I'll miss you, Claude.' Claudia extracted her hands from her pockets and gave Leigh a tight hug.

'Hard to believe they're both gone,' said Claudia uncertainly. 'Not that we were a very close family.'

'I know what you mean. Still, it is strange.'

They were silent for another moment. It was still ten minutes before boarding. Then

Claudia asked, 'Braden will be back soon?'
Leigh nodded.

Leigh had told Claudia that Braden had business in Denver, but she hadn't said what. Perhaps he'd be able to locate Hania's birth certificate. They'd had no trouble getting hold of the birth certificates of the three younger Castle girls in Culver City. The hospital had the records and showed them to Braden, who explained the need to verify their births with regard to their mother's inheritance. But Hania's was not there of course, since she had been born in Denver.

The plane was announced, interrupting Leigh's thoughts. She turned to hug her sister again.

'Well, goodbye, sis,' said Claudia. 'Write when you get back to New York.'

'I will.'

'It'd be great to see you more often.'

Leigh fidgeted with her hands. 'I know.' She had come close to telling Claudia about her discovery last evening, but something kept her from it. Perhaps because she didn't want Claudia to postpone returning to work on her account. She knew Claudia would stay if she thought Leigh needed her help. Or perhaps the matter was just too personal to share, even with a close sister. 'You'd better go.'

'Yes.' Claudia hooked the strap of her tote bag over over shoulder and walked toward the door. She pushed it open and, with a wave, went on through.

Leigh watched through the glass of the small county airport as the wind whipped around Claudia, mussing her short dark hair, billowing her jacket behind her.

When she and Leigh had been younger, they had confided with glee about the men in their lives. Leigh remembered huddling on the bed talking for hours. Even in later years, they had often called each other long-distance to talk about personal problems. Why then did Leigh feel reluctant to talk to Claudia about Braden now? Was it because she was afraid her relationship with Braden would come to nothing? That something she had never foreseen might stand between them?

She forced the nausea down in her stomach and watched the plane move slowly away from the airport. The uncertainties of the last two weeks hovered over them still. The plane taxied to the end of the runway and revved its motors. Leigh waited as the pilot got his signals, then gathered speed for takeoff. Slowly the silver plane sailed up toward the jagged peaks. It was such a tiny plane, it was lost in the clouds in minutes.

She pulled her jacket around her and

turned to go, her thoughts rambling. In the gravel parking lot outside, she opened the door to the Datsun, which she'd borrowed from Hania to drive Claudia to the airport. When they'd come down this morning, her rented Mustang had had a flat. There hadn't been time to change it and still get Claudia to the airport, so Hania insisted they take her car.

Hania declined to accompany them. She must have sensed that Leigh would like to see Claudia off alone. Hania knew that the two younger women had always been close. Or was it merely embarrassment over the inheritance? Leigh bit her lip. Drat Sybil for causing this rift in the family.

She backed up to pull out of the parking area toward the local highway that would take her back to town. Suddenly she felt lonely; now there was only Hania left to talk to, and they seemed to have little to say to one another. Perhaps she ought to try harder, Leigh thought. Hania was obviously unhappy, muzzled as she was by Nathan. Perhaps if she got Hania alone — when Nathan was at the bank.

Funny, thinking about Hania. She used to laugh more. She had always been quiet, yes, but in her own private way, she had seemed to accept her responsibilities with a light heart.

Leigh tapped the steering wheel with her thumb, thinking of the family life she had missed these last years. True, she had studied in Europe and developed the survival methods one needed to live in New York. But she had missed out on the day-to-day events in her sisters' and mother's lives. That time couldn't be relived. She couldn't help but feel, though, that if she'd been around her family more during the last few years she would better understand the present mystery.

Then again, perhaps not. What Sybil did may not have had anything to do with recent years. Leigh had asked Claudia what she thought might have changed in Sybil's life to make her disinherit her younger children, but Claudia had been equally mystified.

Leigh took the curve that led into the first town this side of the airport. She remembered passing this industrial town many times as a girl. It was on the way to an old abandoned fort where they used to have picnics.

She crested the hill and picked up speed, coasting down the other side. There was a steep curve at the bottom, and Leigh's foot touched the brake as she was almost there.

Her heart went to her throat as the brake pedal caught, then slipped, and her foot went all the way to the floor. The car swung crazily to the right as she tried to keep control, furiously pumping the brakes, but they were clearly gone. She stopped breathing. Only then did she think to try the emergency brake, but when she did, nothing happened.

Tires screeched, and she swung the wheel back to the left, just missing the gully on the right side before the road leveled out again. It was fairly straight even now, and she gripped the wheel with all her strength as the car plunged forward.

Trees loomed up, then another curve, and Leigh gritted her teeth, certain that she was about to smash into something. There was a field to the left and some barbed wire. Fear clutched her, and she felt the blood drain from her face. A school bus stood dead ahead, letting out a group of small children. She could see its flashing red lights and the children's red and yellow rain slickers as they hopped off the bus and stood in a group at the edge of the road. She hit the horn desperately, and everything seemed to blur.

She felt the horror of what was about to happen and suddenly willed that she die rather than hit one of the children. In seconds that took on magnified importance, she could see them jumping down and pointing, like a movie with no sound.

'No,' gasped Leigh.

The car wasn't going quite as fast now, but

there was still no way to stop it. She swung hard to the left to avoid the bus and prayed that the children were all on the opposite side. The car lurched across the road, dipped into the gully on the left side and plowed to a stop, with its fender buried in the mud. Tall grass waved crazily in front of her.

She turned off the ignition, then closed her eyes and laid her head on the steering wheel. A few minutes later, a tapping noise brought her back to reality. Someone was opening the car door.

'Are you all right, miss?' A frightened-looking man with a gray-green jacket was looking in at her, his hand reaching out, afraid to touch her. 'Do you need a doctor?'

She looked up at the driver from the school bus, dazed. She tried to move. 'I think I'm all right,' she managed to say. Her voice sounded like it came from a great distance, from a long tunnel. 'My brakes went out,' she went on. Her voice shook uncontrollably.

Then, looking toward the bus, 'The children.' Neither of them moved.

'Yes, ma'am. You swerved just in time. They're all right. Are you sure you should move?'

Leigh was already climbing out of the car to stand in the gully, her legs shaking and her heart pounding furiously in the aftermath of fear. The car would have to be towed.

She stood shakily on the shoulder of the road while the bus driver fussed over her. From the windows of the bus, twenty pairs of eyes stared at her in silence, stone still now with their own fright. When they saw that she was moving, they began to bounce up and down in their seats and point, their voices muted by the closed window. She still had the odd sensation of a silent film.

She dared not think what might have occurred if she hadn't swerved in time. She turned to stare at the battered Datsun in horror. What had happened to the brakes? She would have a mechanic check them. Why had they gone out at just that moment? A cold, grim feeling passed over as the idea took hold. This was no accident. Impossible to confront, but somehow a gruesome reality. Someone must have tampered with those brakes to cause the accident.

'I'm really OK,' she told the solicitous bus driver as she re-examined her arms and shoulders. She just wanted to be away from here. It was all she could do to keep from being violently ill.

'Come on to the bus, then. I'll give you a ride into town. You should see a doctor just in case. Then you'll need to have that car towed.'

She rode in the bus with the children into

Culver City. The little faces still stared at her, and some of them whispered, hands covering their mouths. The driver dropped the last of his flock at the bottom of the hill that led to the house. Then the bus groaned on the incline as it took her up to the front gates.

She thanked him and, with wobbly legs, walked to the drive. As she went through the gates, she spotted Carlos fixing the flat on her Mustang. She eyed him warily, wondering what other skills he might have. But why would he . . .

Then it struck her that she had had the accident in Hania's car. Suppose Hania had been driving? Was she the target?

'Oh, no,' she whispered to herself. Was it happening at last? The fate that Braden had predicted? Her heart beat faster as she stared at the dark red house that seemed to cast a long shadow on the hill below. What if someone had tampered with Hania's car intending to harm Hania, not Leigh? No one could possibly know that Leigh would borrow the car . . . unless he had also caused her flat. Then again, it had been Hania herself who suggested Leigh take her car.

She hugged herself. She mustn't let fear dictate her actions now. She forced herself to walk up to the house and tell Hania and Nathan what had happened.

14

Leigh brought her coffee into the living room and sat down on the sofa. She sipped the hot drink slowly, studying her mother's portrait. She felt closer to knowing what Sybil knew. As if she had all the pieces but one, and with that one, the rest would fall into place.

When Leigh had told Nathan and Hania of her accident, their reactions were much as she'd expected. Hania had paled, and Leigh suspected that she realized it might have been meant for her.

'I'm sorry, Hania,' Leigh had said. 'I don't mean to frighten you, but the car must be towed.'

'Of course,' said Hania, glancing in Nathan's direction.

He frowned and rubbed his chin with his fingers. Leigh couldn't help but feel he was hardly concerned at all. But Leigh realized she was biased. Only a lack of proof prevented her from pronouncing her verdict before the jury was in.

'I'll take care of it,' Nathan said. 'Good thing no one was hurt. It could've . . . ' He let it go, averting his eyes from his wife's gaze.

Had Nathan planned the accident himself? Leigh wondered. Would he stoop so low? She had already decided he might have killed Anastasia to keep her out of the way. Now if Hania died, Nathan would get full control of the inheritance.

But what could Leigh say to Hania? That she might not be safe from her own husband? Leigh knew that Hania would never believe her. Loyalty ran too deep in her blood. She would not leave Nathan for any reason, so there was nothing Leigh could do.

Now Leigh sat on the sofa, turning over events in her mind. She remembered one item no one had really looked into. Anastasia's rented Lincoln, or one that looked very much like it, had been in the parking lot at the Cliff Dwellings the day Leigh and Braden had taken their hike along the trail. But she and Braden had not seen Anastasia. If that had been her car, what was she doing there?

Could she have gone there before she went to the mine? Such offbeat places were of interest to the tourists, but hardly to a woman of Anastasia's temperament. The phone rang. Leigh stood.

'I'll get it,' she said. She walked to the hall table to pick it up.

'Is Mrs. Hunter there? This is Berne

Gordon at the garage.'

'Oh, this is Leigh Castle.' She glanced quickly at the living room and then turned away. 'Can I help you? My sister is out.'

'Oh,' he said. 'Well, tell her I have an estimate on the damage done to her car. She'll need to contact her insurance company before I start. There might be a problem.' He sounded doubtful that he should tell anyone but the car's owner.

'You can tell me the problem, Berne,' she said, thinking fast. 'I was driving the car when the accident happened. If it's my fault . . . '

Her ploy worked. 'Oh, no, Miss Castle, it wasn't the driver's fault. The brakes lines had been cut.' Then he stopped, probably aware that he shouldn't have told anyone but Hania.

'Thank you,' she said. 'I'll see that Hania calls you as soon as — ' She broke off as Nathan appeared at the door. 'As possible,' she finished.

'Who was that?' he asked, frowning at the phone as she replaced it in its cradle.

'Berne Gordon at the garage about the car,' she said. 'He asked for Hania, but then his boss interrupted him. She's to call him in half an hour to get the estimate.'

She turned from his gaze and walked up the staircase, pretending she couldn't care

239

less if Nathan's eyes felt like daggers in her back.

★ ★ ★

Denver's air was sharp and clear as the tires of the Boeing 707 bit sharply into the tarmac on landing. Flicking a bit of lint from his gray serge suit, Braden waited until the other passengers gathered their belongings and then disembarked. Only his eyes revealed his brooding concern that he should have brought Leigh with him. How could he be sure she would be safe in Culver City when he still did not have the answers to this mystery? And he would not be back home until late the next night.

He strode purposefully through the jet way, then claimed his baggage. Working his way through a crowd at the curb, he took the next available taxi. Tossing his garment bag into the back seat, he got in and closed the door against the sharp gusts of cold wind that had descended on the mile-high city.

The cab accelerated onto Martin Luther King Boulevard and then onto Colorado Boulevard, but Braden scarcely saw the passing houses. In a few minutes, they were passing the Museum of Natural History, set back on a rise of brown grass.

Now they turned onto Seventeenth Street. Here the houses were old — brick and stone structures reminiscent of the thirties and earlier. Ten minutes later they passed through Cheesman Park, then the cab pulled into the circular driveway of a 1907 mansion built in Second Renaissance style. The gray brick and classical details reflected the taste of the owner, a man who had attended law school with Braden's father, Judge Thomas Humboldt. The judge had listened to Braden's story late the night before on the telephone and agreed to cooperate.

Braden pulled the garment bag out of the cab, paid the driver and mounted the steps to the pillared front porch. A maid in uniform opened the door.

'Mr. Lancaster?' she said. 'Come in. The judge is expecting you.'

She took the garment bag from him and led him to a door that opened onto a study tastefully furnished in dark mahogany. As Braden stepped onto the midnight-blue wool carpet, a gray-haired man with a bushy mustache rose from a stuffed red leather chair. He spread his arms as he crossed the room.

'Braden, my boy,' he said, 'it's good to see you.'

They shook hands and the judge clapped

241

Braden on the back, ushering him into the room.

'I appreciate your helping me out,' said Braden.

'From what you said on the phone, I think your actions are warranted. Now, what can I get you?'

'Nothing, thank you, Judge.'

'How about dinner here?'

'That would be fine. I'll just check into the hotel and then — '

'You're not still talking about a hotel, are you? Effie has made up a room for you, and it would be my pleasure if you would stay here.'

'Well . . . ' said Braden, not wanting to hurt his feelings.

'I promise not to keep you up too late talking tonight.'

Braden smiled in spite of his worries. 'All right then. Thank you for your hospitality.'

'Now,' said the judge, clearing his throat. 'About that court order. I have it right here.' He walked to his desk and opened a drawer.

'I really appreciate this, Judge.'

He waved aside the thanks. 'I think you're doing the right thing. It seems justified to me in the circumstances.'

It had only taken a half-hour on the telephone to convince him. Braden thanked providence that Judge Humboldt was one of

those rare men who could evaluate circumstances rather than sink into a morass of red
tape. Law was often more of a hindrance than
a help, especially in situations like this. But
Braden had been lucky. Now if only his luck
held.

★   ★   ★

The next morning Braden walked through
the electronically activated doors of St.
Luke's Hospital. The receptionist directed
him to the administrator's office.

Mrs. Erika Hansen was a tall woman with
gray hair, all business. 'Please sit down,' she
said, indicating a chair in front of her desk.

Braden handed her the court order
provided by Judge Humboldt, and she put on
the glasses that had been hanging around her
neck when he came in. She studied the
document silently, and Braden got the idea
she had seen similar papers before.

She finished reading and looked up. 'You
may not have expected this, Mr. Lancaster,
but the birth certificate is no longer here.'

'But when I spoke to you on the phone — '

She raised a hand to stop him. 'She was
born here. That is correct. But the papers are
no longer in my hands.'

'Then where are they?' He was getting

243

impatient. It had been a long process of elimination to finally discover which hospital Hania had been born in — now this.

She handed him a card. Penlo Adoption Agency, it said. His pulse leaped. *Adopted.* They had suspected she might have been born out of wedlock, but this put things in a different light altogether.

'I see,' he said.

'I've already telephoned Mrs. Duhurst at the agency. When you told me Judge Humboldt was giving you a court order, I only had to verify it to assure her you have the right to see the papers. I see that you do.'

He rose at the same time she did, and she saw him to the door of her office. He thanked her again for being so cooperative and then found his way to the hospital entrance. Adoptions were kept so hush-hush these days that if he hadn't gotten that court order, he would never have gotten this far. He'd taken the precaution of doing so in advance, knowing that the hospital might not be so willing to show their records in any case.

The cab left him in front of a three-story prewar building on East Fifteenth Street, the bottom floor of which served as the offices for the Penlo Adoption Agency.

He rang the buzzer and was let in. A plump, silver-haired lady in her fifties stood up from behind a desk at the far side of a comfortable lobby done in dark woods and pale-salmon-colored walls. He crossed to her, meeting her formal smile, which lifted a rose mouth and wrinkled the skin around her blue eyes.

'I'm Braden Lancaster. I believe Mrs. Duhurst is expecting me.'

'Oh, yes, Mr. Lancaster. I'll show you the way.'

The receptionist left her post and led Braden through a door and down a hallway of the same color as the lobby. After passing three doors, she slowed and turned right into an office.

Another desk and another woman, younger this time by ten years, and less plump. But with the same professional smile. He gave her one of his own.

'Braden Lancaster,' he said, putting out his hand.

'Oh, yes, Mr. Lancaster. I'm Eleanor Duhurst. Please come in.'

After shaking his hand, Mrs. Duhurst resettled herself at her desk, the loose folds of her peach-colored silk dress falling gracefully.

She glanced over the court order, but evidently Mrs. Hansen had been speaking truthfully when she said that the adoption agency was expecting him and knew the court order to be valid. She handed him an envelope.

'Here are the records,' she said.

He thanked her, taking the envelope she offered. Then he unwound the string that fastened the forty-six-year-old file and withdrew the contents. He flipped through the adoption records to look first at the negative photostat of Hania's birth certificate. The print was faded, but the white letters of the manual typewriter were clear enough. He stopped breathing as he read the names printed there.

Mother, Anna Morgan, the document said. Then, stamped in a space beside the father's name, was the word *unknown*.

He swore to himself. Aloud, to Mrs. Duhurst, he said, 'I'm sorry. This is a surprise.'

'These records are confidential of course,' she said. 'But I understand it was necessary for you to look at them.'

He wasn't listening. Hania had been adopted — by Sybil herself. It was too much to believe. They had it the wrong way around. He stared stonily in front of him for a few minutes.

'Is there anything else?' Mrs. Duhurst's voice brought him back to the present. He rose swiftly.

'No, no. Thank you.'

He exited as quickly as possible, striding back along the salmon-colored hallway. Hania's father was unknown. Why had Sybil and Hawthorne adopted her? Leigh and Braden had suspected that Sybil had had an illegitimate child, out of character as that may have seemed. But instead, Sybil had adopted a servant's child. Out of sheer generosity? Hardly likely. The explanation was all too obvious. Hania must have been Hawthorne's child, not Sybil's. He, Braden, must have been blind not to see it. But if so, why the inheritance?

Certainly it was typical in a marriage of the kind he suspected Sybil and Hawthorne had for Hawthorne to have taken his amorous intentions elsewhere, especially if Sybil was as unreceptive as Leigh described her. Braden could picture the lusty man in the arms of a willing maid. The faded photograph from the attic came to mind. The strange handwriting. It might have been Anna's.

But it was still perplexing. Would Hawthorne have been able to force his own wife to adopt his bastard? Why not give the child up for adoption anonymously? And again, what kind of a gesture had Sybil been trying to make by leaving her legacy to the child she must have fiercely resented?

He glanced at his watch. He would have to call Leigh from the airport. He asked the receptionist to call a taxi. When it pulled up, he got in and gave Judge Humboldt's address.

★ ★ ★

'Hania,' said Leigh as they moved to the living room to drink their coffee. Lunch was over, and Nathan had returned to work.

'Yes, Leigh.'

'Do you ever get . . . ' She hesitated, pursing her lips. 'Lonely,' she finished.

Hania picked up her needlepoint and sat on the brocade sofa, 'Well,' she said noncommitally, 'sometimes. But Nathan and I, we have a way of life, you know.' She threw Leigh a nervous smile, then bent her head closer to the needlework. Leigh set her cup on the coffee table opposite her and sat down near the windows. Seeing that Hania didn't want to talk, she picked up a book, but only stared at the pages. Braden had called from the Denver airport when she'd been out, and she'd just missed him. His connection in Albuquerque was tight, and she doubted she'd hear from him until he got in later.

She noticed that Hania had seemed jittery since Leigh had told her about the near

248

accident with the bus. And now they knew the brake lines had been cut, for Nathan had called the garage back. Suspecting that he would not want to involve the sheriff in this, Leigh had phoned the sheriff herself. He had gone right down to the garage to question the mechanic thoroughly.

But when it came down to it, who could have tampered with the brakes? Most of the family were gone now, and Leigh found it appalling to think that her older sister would have caused the accident. And Leigh had only realized she would need the car an hour before she had left to take Claudia to the airport. So if Hania or Nathan, or anyone else for that matter, had fixed the brakes, when would they have done it?

It was conceivable that Nathan was responsible. After all, he had been displeased to find Leigh snooping around in the west wing that day. Maybe he'd come to view Leigh as a threat and wanted her out of the way.

It was also possible that the damage had been done some time before. It could have been Anastasia's handiwork. Leigh had come to realize more and more just what Anastasia might have been capable of. She had seen it in the hostile glint of her late sister's eyes, though she had been unwilling to acknowledge that until recently.

Leigh also remembered the night she had heard someone about the house, only to find Richard in the library. Had Anastasia or someone else been arranging the accident then? Richard? He might have been outside either before or after their conversation in the library. And whom were they aiming to eliminate?

If Anastasia had tampered with the car, no one would ever know. And Richard was no longer here to question. An uneasy feeling passed over Leigh as she thought about these two. Anastasia had been very upset when she found out she wasn't getting anything from the will. Leigh remembered speculating that perhaps she and Richard were living above their means and were desperate for money. So desperate they would kill?

Leigh stared into her cup. Anastasia, a potential murderer. Yes, that would fit. It was the only thing that did. She had always had a selfish nature, egged on by Sybil. Leigh wasn't sure what, but something in the past had turned Anastasia against the world. Maybe Sybil herself had taught Anastasia to see things that way. Anastasia was certainly capable of killing. And it would have made more sense to find Hania's body at the mine, or at the Cliff Dwellings, instead of Anastasia's.

Leigh raised her head and stared across at Hania, then continued her glance upward to Sybil's portrait at the end of the room. The light seemed to fade as she looked back at her eldest sister, the high temples, the wide, flat cheekbones, light colored curls framing the modest face that was bent over her work. Her heart missed a beat.

Oh, God, why hadn't she thought of it before? She lowered her head quickly, afraid she would give her thoughts away. As soon as she was sure she wouldn't arouse Hania's suspicion, she rose, made an excuse and hurried up to her room.

[Journal Entry]   **March 17, 1941**

Confrontation with Anna. Wants us to take the child. He swears he hasn't seen Anna since I became a wife to him. I believe him. Convinced me the child is innocent. If we take the child, the mother will go away, never know where we've gone. Hawthorne agreed not to keep company with Charlie outside of business. I blamed him for Hawthorne meeting Anna. I don't think he would have known her if it hadn't been for Charlie. Had to take the child. My guilt too. If I hadn't refused Hawthorne in the beginning, maybe she wouldn't have had the child. I wonder if I will like the child.

— S.C.

15

The next morning Leigh had a late breakfast, then went back upstairs.

Braden had returned the evening before and told her what he'd learned. It fit with what she had realized yesterday by comparing Hania with Sybil's portrait. Many pieces were beginning to fall into place, and Leigh and Braden had formulated a theory, which they only needed to prove. They needed to reconstruct what had occurred that day at the mine.

The house was quiet. Nathan was at work. Hania had gone shopping. Mrs. Garcia was busy in the kitchen, and the maids weren't due to clean upstairs until afternoon. Carlos was cutting away dead branches from a tree at the far edge of the property. Free to move about, Leigh went into the room that Anastasia and Richard had stayed in. It had been cleaned and the bed freshly made. Even the ashes were gone from the fireplace. But Leigh had no time to admire the large bedroom with its satin bedspread and velvet chairs. She caught her reflection in the large mirror over the mantel and started. Then she studied her face.

'Yes,' she murmured to herself, turning her head this way and that. 'It ought to do.'

As she opened the armoire, she found what she had hoped for. Some of her late sister's clothes were still there. On inspection, she also found that Anastasia's cosmetics had been left on the dressing table. Quickly she loaded the tote bag she had brought from her own room.

As she was about to shut the armoire door, she glanced down. Next to the pair of shoes she had taken out was the corner of a leather binding. She knelt and reached in to push aside the handbags that partially covered it.

Her hand trembled as she pulled forward a leather volume exactly like the ones upstairs in the attic and the one she'd read. She didn't have to open it to know that it covered the month Hawthorne died and the year following. In an instant, a number of questions were answered. Anastasia had taken it out of the attic, probably the night Leigh had heard someone up there. It was very likely she had also removed the birth certificates from the metal box at the same time. She had either known something or been trying to find it out, and whatever that knowledge was had probably gotten her killed.

But Leigh had no time to verify her

suspicions now. She looked at her watch. Braden would be here soon.

She didn't have long to wait. He pulled up to the house, and she opened the door for him. He kissed her quickly on the lips.

'All set?' he asked.

She nodded, pointing to the bag. Braden glanced behind her, but Leigh shook her head. 'No one's here,' she said.

They hurried to the car and drove back to Braden's house. She went alone to his bedroom and took out some of the cosmetics from the tote bag while Braden made some lunch. She took her time. Everything had to be perfect, and there was no need to rush now. Her face must be made up perfectly to achieve the effect they wanted. In the kitchen, they ate omelettes and a lettuce and cucumber salad. Leigh was nervous, but she knew she should eat.

At two o'clock, Braden placed a call to Hania while Leigh stood with him beside the kitchen phone. They were counting on Hania being alone, with Nathan still at work.

'Hania, this is Braden Lancaster.' His voice was smooth, non-threatening. Leigh watched him, admiring his professional manner, hoping it inspired confidence now. Of course she didn't know if their suspicions were correct, but they had agreed that this was the

255

only way to find out.

'I wonder if I could see you in a half-hour,' he went on. 'There's something else I need to go over with you. Just a few more details.'

He waited, then, 'No, no. I'll pick you up. I have another appointment, and if you wouldn't mind a short ride, I can explain it in the car. It will save me some time.' He put it in such a way that Leigh knew Hania could not refuse.

'Good. I'll see you in forty minutes. I'll have you back before Nathan gets home from work. See you soon.'

As he hung up the phone, he took a deep breath and let it out slowly. 'So far, so good. Let's go.'

Being careful not to muss her hair or dress, Leigh followed Braden out to the car. She knew she would have to wait for a while alone, but she wasn't worried — only nervous, like an actor must be before going on stage. But she mustn't let her fear drive her over the edge. There was too much at stake now. She had to trust Braden. It had been a good idea, and soon they would know everything. For Hania would supply the missing piece.

They drove out of town, past the cemeteries. Two of their number rested there now. How peacefully? Leigh wondered. She shuddered at the irony as they left the cemeteries behind.

At the entrance to the road leading to the mine, Leigh's skin began to feel clammy. This had been the scene of her sister's death. Even if Anastasia deserved it, she had still been a sister. They were carried in the same womb. Unlike Hania, she thought with a shiver. She still found it hard to believe that her own family had become embroiled in such strange doings. A skeleton in her own family's closet. More than one, perhaps.

The Wagoneer rolled to a stop, and Braden got out. Leigh followed, careful not to stumble on the rocks.

'This is the spot, I think,' said Braden.

Leigh nodded as the picture of her dead sister rose up like a phantom, making her feel dizzy. The place was filled with the presence of a violent death. If they meant to frighten Hania, they would surely do it here. The goose bumps rose on Leigh's arms as she contemplated her part.

They surveyed their surroundings. Across the road was the excavation. One step too far could be fatal.

'There, that's the obvious place to wait.' Braden pointed to a half-fallen shack about ten yards from the spot where Anastasia had most likely crossed the road and met her death. They walked toward it. He tested the remaining walls. 'Stay outside, don't lean on anything,' he said.

Then he came to her and took her gently in his arms. 'Be careful,' he said. 'I'll be back soon.'

'I know. Now go on, or you'll mess up my makeup.'

'All right. You know what to do?' He sounded nervous, but she knew the look he gave her was meant to be reassuring.

'Yes,' she said, starting to tremble a little. Her part wasn't much really, and she only had to say one word.

She looked at her watch. Anastasia's watch, really. She had found it on the dresser with the other accessories that had been returned after Anastasia was prepared for burial. Anastasia had died at this time of day, within one or two hours, Leigh thought, still looking at the watch.

Braden left her and hurried back to the car. Overhead the sky was clear. Had it been clear that day? It had rained a little when she and Braden had driven home from the Cliff Dwellings. Anastasia had most likely been there ahead of them, looking for a place to stage her coup. But they had seen other tourists on the trail that day. She had probably decided the place wasn't secluded enough for what she had in mind and come here instead.

Leigh smoothed her skirt, Anastasia's skirt. Her hair was molded the way Anastasia had worn hers, and Leigh knew that with her makeup heavier than she usually wore it, there would be a good likeness. They both had their mother's narrow cheekbones. And the scarf around her neck was the same . . .

It was too gruesome to contemplate. She didn't need to resemble Anastasia dead, but rather alive. Not that she would pass for her late sister upon close examination; it was only the illusion they wanted. And it only had to last for a moment. At Braden's she had practiced Anastasia's walk. Everything was ready.

She heard tires on gravel and pulled back near the shack. The shadows would hide her until it was time. Soon she heard Braden's voice.

'It was over here, wasn't it?' he asked Hania. His tone was light, easy, as if he only wanted to confirm something for himself, not extract a confession.

Now. Feeling more like Anastasia than herself, Leigh moved forward into the light, confronting Hania, who stood still, staring. Leigh gestured as she had seen Anastasia do, then she walked forward, Hania's name on her lips.

A cry escaped Hania's throat, her hands

over her eyes as she fell backward. 'No,' she shrieked.

Braden was there to catch her, and they eased her to a sitting position on the ground, safely away from the excavation. Hania still screamed, her fists tightened.

'No, no. She's come back. I didn't mean to do it, Anastasia. I didn't mean it. I didn't push her, really. I swear I didn't touch her.' She clutched at Braden, her words pouring out.

'She made me do it. I didn't mean to kill her. Tell them. Tell them it was an accident.'

Leigh looked over her sister's head at Braden. They had gotten what they wanted, but at what cost? She reached for Hania, afraid they might have driven her too far toward the breakdown that had so obviously been threatening all along.

'It's all right, sis, it's all right,' said Leigh, her voice soothing. 'Can you tell us what happened?'

But Hania shrank into Braden, her eyes wide with fright.

'It's not Anastasia, it's me, Leigh,' she said slowly, her words attempting to penetrate Hania's hysteria.

She took her sister's shoulders and shook her. 'Look at me, Hania. I'm Leigh.'

Hania's face, drained of color, looked back

with unbelieving eyes, and Leigh was petrified by what they'd done to her. But then Hania lurched forward, sobbing into Leigh's shoulder. The words began to pour out — as if they had been held in too long.

'Sh — she made me come here — she said she had something to talk to me about,' Hania said, her breath heaving. 'She said she couldn't tell me at the house, someone might hear. And if I didn't come, she'd show something to the family I wouldn't like. She said she knew things even I didn't know but that I'd want to find out.'

Now Hania cried like a baby instead of the older, responsible sister she'd always been, and she clung to Leigh for dear life.

Leigh nodded, cradling Hania's shoulders. She seemed to be over the worst of it now. Her sobbing slowed, and Leigh knew she would find relief in talking. Leigh and Braden listened intently as the story came out more slowly, and she blew her nose on the handkerchief Braden gave her, though when she glanced up at him, there was still fear in her eyes.

'I'm sorry, sis,' Leigh said, striving to hang on to Hania's sanity. It was important that she talk now — that she tell them everything.

Finally, Hania's breathing became more controlled. She looked at her hands as she struggled with the words.

'I told Nathan I was going shopping, only I came out here with her. She was there, just like you were. Oh, Leigh, I thought it was her. I thought she'd come back.' She stopped, pressing her lips together and shutting her eyes as she took several deep breaths.

'I know,' whispered Leigh, smoothing Hania's hair. 'I'm sorry I frightened you.'

Hania blew her nose again. 'It's all right. I wanted to tell someone anyway. I really did.' She glanced up helplessly.

'Go on,' Braden said gently.

'She had an envelope in her hands and gave it to me. It was my birth certificate. I didn't believe her at first, but it showed that Mother wasn't my . . . ' She stopped and fingered the neck of her dress. 'That my mother was another woman, Anna Morgan. I wasn't Sybil's daughter at all.'

'I know, darling. We found that out.' Anna Morgan was Hawthorne's mistress. Hawthorne had asked Sybil to adopt Anna's child. Perhaps Anna threatened to create a scandal. It all fit now — Sybil's reluctance to marry, her dislike of giving herself to her husband. Obviously, Hawthorne sought his pleasure elsewhere, and Cousin Charlie arranged that he and Hawthorne dally with the maids.

'Anastasia said she knew,' murmured

Hania. Her words were hesitant now, as if she were once more a shy girl, begging for acceptance. Her eyes were distant, as if she remembered the horror of it all.

'She said she'd known all along. She'd heard them fighting about it. They didn't know she was listening. She was supposed to be in bed, you see.'

'And you were there too,' she said to Leigh. 'Anastasia had brought you downstairs for some milk, but all you did was stand in the hall and cry. Mother accused Father of watching out for me more than for the others because I wasn't her child.'

Hania fell silent, shaking her head slowly.

'Then she remembered later,' said Braden.

Hania nodded. 'She remembered the name Sybil had thrown at him that night. Mother cursed Anna Morgan, and Hawthorne for ever knowing her.'

Leigh threw Braden a surprised look. She had been there herself? But she must have been too young to know what the arguing was about. In any case, she didn't remember. She turned her attention back to Hania.

It must have been unsettling to find out after all these years that she was illegitimate and that Sybil, who was not even her own mother, had not only brought her up but left her the entire estate.

'I told Anastasia I didn't care,' said Hania, sitting up straighter. 'I told her I was going to give up the inheritance. I didn't want my sisters holding a grudge against me for the rest of my life.'

'But Nathan didn't want you to?' Braden asked.

She nodded, swallowing. 'He told me to wait and think it over. He wanted to be cautious, you know. He wanted to protect the money. Our money,' she finished in a small voice.

Then she regained her confidence. 'Anastasia didn't want to listen. She wanted to blackmail me for half of the inheritance. She said Nathan would never want a scandal, and that she could make one if I didn't agree. She would spread it around that I was illegitimate. She knew Nathan wouldn't like that. He would make it hard for me.

'She frightened me, saying that if I didn't survive, the money would go to you all anyway. She looked mean. Oh, Leigh, she looked so mean.' She sobbed silently as Leigh comforted her.

'All right, Hania. She's not here anymore. Tell us the rest.'

'I thought she meant to kill me then and there. I was standing near the edge of the road here, and she was coming closer.' Hania started to shake. She looked up at Leigh with a pleading look in her eyes.

'Oh, Leigh, she wanted to kill me. I could feel it. I've never felt such evil. She reached out to push me. I stumbled. I thought I'd fall in. All I meant to do was get away from her. I was afraid. I don't know how it happened. She was calling me names. I screamed at her and lunged away, but she lost her footing and fell. I guess it was my fault for not trying to help her when I stumbled, but I didn't.'

Hania started to cry again, but it was clear she wanted to get it all out. She went on. 'I saw her head fall forward and hit the rocks. The papers' — she paused — 'the birth certificate fell in. I was glad when I saw it go down there.' She looked toward the pit. 'She was dead.'

Leigh could imagine the terror Hania had felt. She could imagine Anastasia, vicious, greedy Anastasia, going at Hania, threatening her, driving her toward the edge.

Leigh cradled her sister. 'It's all right, Hania. We know what happened now. It's just between us. Braden and I guessed the truth, but we agreed that if you told us, we'd keep your secret. You're not a murderer, Hania. It was an accident.'

Hania looked up at Braden, her voice cracked now and old sounding. 'I'm glad I told you. I couldn't live with it any longer. I want to tell the others. I can't live with this on my conscience.'

Braden looked at Leigh and then back at Hania. 'It's your choice, Hania. I'm glad you want to clear it up. I believe we can prove that Anastasia threatened you and that it was an accidental death, just like the coroner said.'

They were quiet for a few moments as they helped Hania to her feet. Leigh had hoped for this outcome. She realized they might need additional evidence and had suggested to Braden that the Hazletts' bank account and business dealings could be investigated. It might prove that they had a reason to need money. Hania ought to have no trouble being acquitted of any wrongdoing.

The light was fading. Somewhere a twig snapped, and a blue jay fluttered between some branches of a dead tree. A breath of wind teased the strands of hair that fell across Leigh's face. She turned slowly, and they walked to the Wagoneer. Braden held the door while Hania got in, then Leigh. She clutched her sister's hand as they returned to town.

16

Braden Lancaster faced Richard Hazlett across the length of Hazlett's study. Floor-to-ceiling bookshelves were filled with leather-bound volumes, but even from his vantage point near the marble fireplace, he could see that on many, the bindings had never been cracked. The English country house was comfortably elegant.

He sipped the sherry Richard had handed him as he watched the other man pace a few steps across the Persian rug. He turned back to Braden.

'You said you wanted to see me about' — he paused — 'my wife.' He rushed the last two words and downed the rest of his glass.

'Yes,' said Braden, walking over to a cherrywood side table and setting his glass down. 'I'm sorry to have to bother you with questions, and of course you don't have to answer any.'

Richard refilled his glass from a crystal decanter. He turned sarcastic. 'Why not? There's nothing to hide. And as to reputation . . . ' He shrugged and tossed down his second glass.

'Do you mind if I ask you some rather personal questions?' said Braden.

'Such as?'

'Did Anastasia tell you what she knew about Hania Hunter?'

'That she was illegitimate? Yes. But I warned her it would be foolish to try to use that information, though at first I thought we might be able to contest the will.'

'Did you know if she planned to?'

'If you mean blackmail, no, she said nothing about it.'

'I see.' Of course, thought Braden. Even if she had, Richard would never say so. It would be the next thing to admitting he was an accomplice.

'Did you think she might try anyway, in spite of your, ah, warning?'

Richard smirked and looked at his glass as if he were considering having a third one. 'I knew my wife, Mr. Lancaster. She was capable of many things.'

'Blackmail?'

'Yes.'

'Murder?'

He raised the glass and studied it. 'But she was the one who died.'

'Yes.' Braden lifted his own glass, but did not drink. He studied the unicorn in a tapestry that hung on one wall devoid of bookshelves. It was poetic justice that Anastasia had died. Dare he suggest that to Richard? No matter.

Richard faced the tapestry. Braden wanted to know more about his relationship with his late wife, but how much would Richard open up? Perhaps the liquor would help.

'I hope you don't mind answering another personal question,' said Braden.

'They're all bound to be personal, aren't they? But ask ahead. As you said, I don't have to answer.'

'It's just that I'd like to be sure of motives — at least as sure as I can be in a case where nothing can really be proven.'

'Then why bother?'

'Call it peace of mind,' said Braden. 'I don't like to leave loose ends. I'd like to know if you and your wife were in any kind of financial bind.'

'You mean, did we need the money from Sybil's estate? Yes, we could have used it.' He gestured at the tasteful surroundings and out the window of the manor house with its manicured grounds.

'Anastasia and I developed a certain life style in London. Of course, she didn't come down here much. She preferred the penthouse in town. But I kept this place because of the quiet. I need that, Mr. Lancaster, more than she did.'

'I see.' He hated to keep pressing the man, but it was his only chance. 'One more thing, then I'll leave you alone, and of course all this is off the record.'

'Obviously.'

'Do you think Anastasia would have threatened Hania in order to convince her to divide up the estate?'

Richard lifted his lips in a sardonic smile. 'You're asking me to pronounce the sentence on my own wife? I will only say this. When she wanted something, she would go to great lengths to get it. As I said, I had no part in whatever she might have done.'

'The car in which Leigh drove her sister to the airport had its brake lines cut. That must have been done the night before. Leigh said she encountered you in the library that night.'

Richard's glance met Braden and he lifted his eyebrows an eighth of an inch. Then he looked away. 'I didn't cut the brake lines, if that's what you mean. I had no reason to cause Leigh's accident.'

'But the accident was meant for Hania. It was her car. Where was your wife that night?'

Richard's eyes darted to the sides of the room. 'I don't know. She came to bed after I did.'

'I see,' said Braden.

Richard walked to an overstuffed chair and placed a hand on the back. 'Anastasia probably cut the brake lines, planning an accident for Hania in case she refused to share the estate and something went wrong at the silver mine. She never said as much of course, but I knew my wife.'

The creases in his temples and across his forehead were witness to his personal burdens, and Braden could appreciate what those words cost him.

'Thank you, Richard. I will not bother you again. I'll see myself out.'

Braden turned toward the tall oak doors and walked through to a hallway with a vaulted ceiling. His footsteps echoed over the marble floor, and when he reached the front steps, he was glad to be out in the sunlight. It was bright for an English day, but not hot like it was in the States. He strolled for a moment near a flower garden, watching the gardeners in the distance bending over sculptured shrubs.

The setting suited Richard Hazlett, Braden thought. He seemed a man of taste and probably did need the solitude of living in the country. He could equally well imagine the penthouse in London, which Anastasia, with her taste for fast living, naturally would have preferred.

As he breathed in the pungent scent of nasturtiums, he realized how eager he was to be away from here.

Braden had accomplished a lot in the last eight months. He had not pressed Leigh, realizing that she needed time to sort out her life, time to make sure she could live with the events that had so strangely brought them together.

And so he had let the months go by, communicating with her by letter and phone. But that was no longer enough. He needed to see her again, wanted to see her again.

★ ★ ★

Leigh watched Braden over her whiskey sour. He was tanned now, and auburn highlights were beginning to show in his dark-brown hair.

He had arrived in New York yesterday, to tie up loose ends, he said. But she knew it was more than that. She knew they had to discuss the future.

Braden turned back to her from watching the passers-by on the sidewalk outside the restaurant on Columbus Avenue. She mused over what he had told her about seeing Richard Hazlett.

'Do you think he told you the truth?'

Richard was a nervous man, and she remembered his bravado had completely broken down at his wife's death.

Braden shrugged. 'How can we be sure? He admitted he wanted the money but swore he knew nothing of Anastasia's plans.'

Braden gazed out the window again at the twinkling lights of Lincoln Center.

'You have a pensive look,' she commented.

He shook his head and grinned at her with that funny smile she had come to love. Her heart turned over. 'I was thinking about how twisted things are,' he said. 'I'm thinking I'm not cut out to be a lawyer.'

'You mean crime doesn't pay? I'm sorry. It wasn't a very good joke.'

'It's all right.'

Leigh realized how much time had passed. Time enough for her to get over all the feelings associated with her mother's and sister's deaths. Life moved on.

He shrugged. 'Too often the real culprit gets off, and innocent people suffer for it. This wouldn't be the first time.'

She looked out at the brightly lighted plaza. In half an hour, the curtain would go up. 'You mean my mother.'

'Yes, I think so.'

'I think so too.'

They were silent for a time, their thoughts

punctuated only by the clinking of glass and the din of voices around them. Finally, Braden spoke.

'Your mother waited a long time for her revenge.'

Leigh nodded. It was true. She had come to the same conclusion. 'Imagine hating Hania all those years,' she said.

'And not being able to do anything about it.'

'Except turning Anastasia against Hania by spoiling her and pointing out continually how Father loved Hania better.'

'Diabolic and clever,' said Braden.

'I can't believe I never suspected,' Leigh said.

Would she ever really understand her mother? A woman saddled with her husband's illegitimate child, hating the child, hating the child's mother. What had Sybil and Hawthorne talked about in private all those years ago that had made Sybil adopt a child she resented so much?

Whatever words had passed between Sybil and Hawthorne on the subject would forever remain their secret. Except for what Anastasia had heard, except for what Sybil had wanted her to hear, and except for what she'd left in the diary. Leigh shook her head. Incredible the lengths people went to in Sybil's day to avoid a scandal. Illegitimate children were swept under the rug, never to be discussed.

Had it been Hawthorne's arrogance that made him want to claim his own? Or a good heart? What emotion had driven him? How bitter for Sybil to have to face, daily, the child who had been carried by her husband's lover. How she must have wanted to turn her back on that part of Hawthorne's life. And yet she never could. But yet hadn't it been her fault too? The diary said she had not welcomed Hawthorne to the marriage bed for some time. Obviously he had gone to Anna then.

'Sybil knew her daughter,' Braden said. 'She hoped Anastasia would seek her revenge.'

'Especially when baited by the will,' said Leigh.

'Yes. It explains everything, doesn't it?'

Leigh knew she didn't have to answer the last question aloud. Yes, it did explain almost everything. It explained how vengeance could be gotten even from the grave.

'I remember meeting Anastasia in the foyer the afternoon of the funeral. You had just left the house. Anastasia asked me if Mother had ever told me anything about Hania, even a long time ago. Anastasia must have been thinking about Hania's illegitimacy and what Mother might have wanted done about it.'

Braden nodded silently.

'Do you think she ever loved him?' Leigh asked after a pause. 'She bore him three children. What could she have felt?'

Braden shrugged and brushed the perspiration from his forehead. 'She was Catholic of course.'

'Yes.' But they would never know the rest.

'I think I'm ready for a walk,' he said, signaling for the check. Outside, the trees moved silently, and leaves danced in the wind.

It was time, she thought, as she rose and lifted her jacket from the back of the chair. Time to wash away the ghosts of the past.

They stood and left the restaurant. He took her arm, and they joined the crowd walking up to Lincoln Center. He stopped her in front of the fountain, and when she looked into his eyes, she knew what was coming. Even before he asked her, she knew what her answer would be, for she had pondered it the past eight months.

'Leigh?' he said, raising his brows in a questioning look. The lights from the fountain reflected in his eyes as he moved his arms around her.

Their lips met, and they held each other, sharing warmth, communicating what words couldn't. Finally he moved his head, and she nestled against his shoulder.

'Will you marry me, darling?' he said, his mouth brushing against her hair.

'Yes,' she said, holding him closer. It was a simple word, but it carried with it the future she had decided upon. She could feel him relax. He held her away to look at her.

'I'm glad you said yes,' he said, and she saw then the worry that had been in his eyes.

'It's over now, isn't it?' she said.

'Yes, darling, and I love you.'

'I know, and I love you.'

They walked slowly across the plaza and people hurried past them to performances that were taking place inside the three buildings that housed New York's finest opera, ballet, and music. Voices and lights celebrated the summer evening. Leigh had something to celebrate now too. She squeezed Braden's arm and looked up at him, smiling.